"I would have remembered someone like you if we'd ever met." Hilda's voice was low, vibrant.

"We've never met," Brenda said, thankful Hilda hadn't mentioned her likeness to Princess Diana, but curious why she skirted her question. "I was at the autograph show this past December in Fort Lauderdale. Unfortunately, I was part of the crowd that watched the commotion between you and Clifford."

Hilda nodded slowly. "Ah, yes, that's where you met Clifford Satterly, I suppose. May I get you something to drink?"

Brenda shook her head. "No, thank you. The charter boat will be back for me in an hour. I'd like to ask you some questions."

Hilda sat down on the couch opposite Brenda and crossed her long legs in a smooth move. She reminded Brenda of a sleek cat.

"Very well, Brenda Strange, we can make this all business if you like." She set her dark gaze directly on Brenda. "The man is a lunatic. I mean it. He frightens me. Clifford's been calling and harassing me almost daily. He gloated about hiring you. That's why I knew you'd be knocking on my door eventually." She stopped and smiled. "And here you are."

Visit

Bella Books

at

BellaBooks.com

or call our toll-free number

1-800-729-4992

THE
MISSING
PAGE

A BRENDA STRANGE MYSTERY

Patty G. Henderson

Bella
BOOKS

2005

Bella Books, Inc.
P.O. Box 10543
Tallahassee, FL 32302

Printed in the United States of America on acid-free paper
First Edition

Editor: Christi Cassidy
Cover designer: Michelle Corby

ISBN 1-59493-004-X

For my Michelle . . . You make it all so much more special.

Acknowledgments

I can't let any book go by without giving a tip of the fedora to my editor, Christi Cassidy. This lady works hard and my greatest appreciation to her.

I love my editor.

P.S.: She really isn't twisting my arm. Honest.

About the Author

Patty G. Henderson has been published since the early 1970s in magazines such as *Paragon* and Dale Donaldson's *Moonbroth*. She's also the author of the Brenda Strange supernatural mystery series. *The Burning of Her Sin* was the first book in the series, which is set in Tampa, Florida. Bella Books published the second book in the series, *Tangled and Dark*. *The Missing Page* continues the Brenda Strange PI series. *Blood Scent*, an erotic lesbian vampire romance, was Henderson's first published book. She has also had short fiction published in mystery and horror anthologies, including Bella Books' *Call of the Dark*.

Between writing novels and short fiction, Patty still works a full-time job at a photography studio. She is a Tampa native who still lives in beautiful South Tampa.

Prologue

Brenda Strange sat on the snow, surrounded only by the icy, shrieking wind. The day had dawned bleak and turned darker still. Tarrytown, New York, was covered in a thin blanket of white. Her mother lay deep in that frozen ground. It was no day to bury your mother.

"Yea, though I walk through the valley of the shadow of death, I will fear no evil, for *you* are with me, your rod and your staff, they comfort me." The priest's baritone voice still echoed in her head.

"Don't worry, Mommy's here with me." Her little brother's voice was barely a whisper in contrast.

"Timmy?"

"Ashes to ashes. Dust to dust." The priest's voice persisted.

She shook her head to get the intruding voice out.

"Timmy?" she called out loud into the cold, her breath making wispy, white clouds that the wind carried away.

Everyone had left once the funeral service ended. Her father, the rest of the family, her friends Cubbie and Eddy, even her lover, Tina. It had been harder getting Tina to leave. Brenda had wanted just a few more minutes alone with her mother.

But Timmy was here too. Her little brother assured her that their mother was now in heaven with him. It was comforting to know that both God and Timmy had forgiven Mother.

"Brendi," her little brother said, "Mommy couldn't have stopped that red car from killing me. God knew. You know."

Brenda didn't. But she forgave her mother in the end. It had been hard to let go of all that resentment. Instead, she watched the wracking pain of cancer torture her mother as it ravaged her body. In humiliation and regret, her mother had begged acceptance from her daughter. And forgiveness.

Brenda shed tears at her mother's death, but they were born of relief, not grief. Brenda had also knocked at death's door and been yanked back. She'd taken that trip and seen the beautiful light that waited at the other end. Brenda was almost jealous of her mother and Timmy. They were already there.

Beneath her, the snow was cold and lumpy. Her father would be waiting at Montepoint, with Tina and the others, a blazing fire in the fireplace and a hot dinner. He'd need her comfort.

Brenda got up slowly, knowing that when she left here, she wouldn't be back again for some time. She walked slowly toward the car, waving one last time to Timmy and the shadowy figure that never quite took form next to him. She waved at her too.

"Good-bye, Mother."

Chapter One

From her office, Brenda heard the phone ring three times at Cubbie's desk before Cubbie answered it.

"Strange Investigations." She sounded out of breath.

Brenda smiled to herself. Cubbie had probably been raiding the refrigerator or in the bathroom. The man's voice on the other end was so loud, Brenda could hear it through the open door of her office. It sounded hostile.

"Hold on one second, Clifford." Cubbie poked her head into Brenda's office. "It's Clifford Satterly. To say he's upset would be an understatement."

"I've got it." Brenda picked up her phone. "This is Brenda Strange."

She remembered the letter Clifford had sent from Spain with all the colorful stamps. It had come shortly after Christmas, just before all hell broke loose. She'd stuffed it with the rest of the mail that had stacked up. Her mother died on February 2. It was mid-

March, and Brenda was just now clawing her way up from the turmoil her mother's passing had created in her life.

"Didn't you get my check?" Clifford rushed the words out. "I don't have much time. You've got to help me." He sounded desperate.

"Calm down, Clifford. I just got back in the office." She wasn't going to go into the why with him. If he'd waited three months to contact her, it couldn't be a matter of life and death. "I haven't had the chance to look into the paperwork you sent."

He breathed hard into the phone. "I don't know how much longer I can wait." His voice trailed off. Was he looking over his shoulder?

"Clifford, are you in trouble? Is there a phone number where I can reach you?" She thought hard and was sure he hadn't given one in the letter.

"They're after me. I can't stay put. I'll call you again. Find the Malenko manuscript, please."

"Clifford, wait. Who's after you?"

Too late. There was a click at the other end of the line and then a dial tone. Brenda hung up and started rummaging through the mail on her desk. She was sure it was there.

"New case, boss lady?" Cubbie was standing at the door.

"It looks like it," Brenda said, distracted, as she dumped envelope after envelope of advertising and credit card invitations in the trash. Peeking from beneath a blue Valpak coupon envelope was the letter with the bright Spanish stamps. "Ah-ha." She held it up to Cubbie.

Cubbie shook her head, unruly red curls bouncing to her shoulders. Brenda had been shocked when she walked in and Cubbie greeted her. It was a rare occasion when her short, round friend didn't wear one of her baseball caps. Cubbie had brushed it off as a "bad hat day."

"Honey, that man on the phone sounded scared. Do you know what you're gettin' into? Are you ready for that?" Her blue eyes looked deep into Brenda's.

4

Brenda smiled, appreciating her concern. "I'm ready, Cubbie. I need the distraction. Don't worry, I know a little about this case."

She pulled out the copies of FedEx receipts and tracking numbers that Clifford Satterly had sent and searched the envelope for a return address. There wasn't one.

Cubbie came in and sat down across from her. "Why is he in such a rush?"

"Tina and I met him in Ft. Lauderdale at one of Eddy's autograph shows. He was in a shouting match with another dealer, Hilda Moran. Apparently, he sent her a rare manuscript she was interested in buying from him. He claims she stole it. She claims she never got it." Brenda looked at the FedEx signature receipt. Hilda Moran's signature was plainly visible.

"You think she stole it?" Cubbie asked.

"She signed for it." Brenda handed her the copy. "The question is, is it her signature?"

Cubbie arched an eyebrow as she scanned the FedEx receipt. "You thinking someone else forged her signature? Who would know the value of this"—she waved her thick hand at Brenda—"this manuscript?"

"The Malenko manuscript," Brenda added as she looked closely at the papers. "I don't know that much about it other than it's one of a kind. Highly sought after by collectors."

Among the papers Clifford had sent, Brenda found a copy of a membership card for the Autographs International Club signed by Hilda Moran. How did he get hold of that? The two signatures looked close enough to be the same.

Brenda flopped the envelope and papers back down on the desk. "I've got to find out who signed for the manuscript. I could track down the FedEx driver who did the actual delivery." She looked at Cubbie, her mind already moving ahead. Questioning Hilda Moran was the first thing she wanted to do if she took the case on, and Hilda lived in Key Largo. "Sound easy, Cubbie?" Brenda smiled. "Find the driver. Get a description of who answered the door and signed for the delivery, have a professional handwriting expert compare the two signatures, then talk to Hilda or maybe some of her neighbors who might have seen anything, and you've got a big chunk of the case solved."

Cubbie scrunched up her eyebrows in thought. Brenda made up her mind before Cubbie could answer.

"I need a vacation. How about you? Why don't you book me at the nicest hotel in Key Largo?" She thought a bit longer on that. If she was going to Key Largo, she wanted something different from the typical four-star hotel. "Find a place closest to the water. Something quaint." Brenda looked at the calendar on her desk. It was only Tuesday. Better to travel on a weekday than a weekend. "Book me through Friday. I can leave tomorrow morning."

Cubbie's mouth made an *O* in surprise. "The Keys?" Her eyes lit up. "Snorkeling? Fishing? I can help with the case," she said in a hopeful voice.

Brenda shook her head. "I need you here. Someone has to take care of business and Butterscotch. I'll make duplicate keys to Malfour House before I leave." Brenda paused, thinking of her kitten, Butterscotch, and of her ghostly companions, Carlotta and Angelique. "The ghosts won't harm you, I promise."

Cubbie had her mouth open, poised to object.

"I'll bring you an alligator baseball cap as a souvenir," Brenda said.

Cubbie closed her mouth and offered Brenda a scowl. "It isn't the same."

The Florida Keys. To Brenda, the words conjured images of magical, tropical islands surrounded by crystal-clear blue waters and soft breezes of perpetual summer even in the lagging days of winter. The perfect beachcomber's life, she thought, free of worry. Her parents had vacationed often in Florida and in the Florida Keys while she had her nose buried deep in schoolbooks and then law tomes. She was a Florida Keys virgin.

The beauty of the islands beckoned. In Brenda's mind, it would have been a sin to fly there and back. She opted instead to drive her vintage 1963 Jaguar convertible the whole distance. Being able to drive her drop top in beautiful weather was one of the reasons she had wanted a move to Florida.

She left shortly after 8 a.m. on Wednesday. If she was lucky, the cold fronts would stay away so she could pop the top down and enjoy the brisk breeze and warming rays of the sun that only a perfect Florida day in March could bring.

Equipped with a South Florida map that covered Miami and the Florida Keys, Brenda chose to take Alligator Alley into Miami, stop at the FedEx Central Hub where all packages originated for delivery to the Keys, then pick up U.S. Highway 1 that snaked through the Keys and all the way down to Key West.

Only minutes into Miami, Brenda felt the claustrophobia set in. The city unsettled her. It was crowded, gaudy and loud. Miami may have palmetto trees, flamingos and pastel Art Deco buildings, she thought, but it was a cheap, painted lady of a town. She wanted to make this visit short.

She got her wish. FedEx would not allow her to question any of their drivers. Apparently, PIs in Miami ranked about as high on the list of desirables as street junkies. If she wasn't with the Miami-Dade Police or Clifford Satterly, the shipper, or Hilda Moran, the addressee, she was out of luck.

Discouraged but not defeated, Brenda thought she'd try to convince Hilda Moran to come to Miami and talk to the driver herself. It's what an innocent person would do.

By 2:30, Brenda was only too happy to leave Miami behind. As soon as she hit U.S. Highway 1, the mile markers appeared, indicating the distance traveled through the Keys. Looking at the map, Brenda figured another hour and a half or maybe two till Key Largo.

The drive was breathtaking with the azure waters of the Atlantic to her left and Gulf of Mexico on her right, but the trip was long. Brenda was stiff and the air slamming her face salty, tinged with a fishy smell. She breathed a sigh of relief when she finally spotted the sign for the Key Largo Casablanca Resort.

Tucked away from the crowded cluster of mom-and-pop motels and cottages, Key Largo Casablanca Resort was a hidden gem. The narrow road came to a dead end directly in front of a collection of quaint, colorful stucco buildings. Beyond them, the brilliant Atlantic glistened and a white sandy beach surrounded by palm trees beckoned. Cubbie had picked the perfect place, definitely out of the way and with an ocean-front view.

Brenda checked into what the registration clerk termed their "premiere cottage." It was only a few feet away from the beach.

Too bad she wouldn't get a chance to enjoy it. She was here on business. The cottage was definitely quaint. The décor was authentic fifties with tropical paintings, bright bedspreads and lamps that Brenda figured hadn't been updated since then. There were ample windows, the Atlantic waters visible in each view.

Brenda pulled out Hilda Moran's phone number that Clifford Satterly had supplied. She pressed the numbers on her cell phone and waited until an answering machine picked up. Hilda's message was short and businesslike. Brenda didn't leave her number. She'd just drive to the address. It shouldn't be hard to find on such a small island, she figured.

When she called the registration desk and asked for directions, the woman on the other end chuckled. Seems Hilda Moran lived on a converted barge permanently docked off the island. A house-boat, for lack of a better name, and the only way to get there was to charter a boat. The woman suggested several charter services.

Brenda sat down on the bed, leaned back and sighed. She'd had enough of boats and adventures in or around water. With the Paula Drakes case behind her, she wanted nothing more to do with diving or boating. She'd done enough swimming in dark waters while being shot at to last a lifetime. But nothing was guaranteed in the private investigation game. You didn't always get what you wanted.

The sun was low outside. Brenda hadn't realized how tired she was. And how hungry. She hadn't stopped for a bite to eat since leaving Malfour. But before even considering food, she wanted to check out the boat charters.

8

Registration recommended Sunny Keys Tours and Dive Boat Charters, but she'd have to wait because Doug Riddle, the owner, was gone for the day. Brenda didn't feel like going on her own hunt for charter boats, so it was time to feed the rumblings in her stomach.

A big fan of the Bogart and Bacall film *Key Largo*, Brenda had been looking forward to eating an early dinner at the same restaurant they shot the film in. The tour books listed it as the Caribbean Club.

When she asked about it at the registration desk, she was surprised at the response. Apparently, it wasn't the glamour spot she had envisioned. They gave her directions and recommended the Cracked Conch for breakfast.

Brenda decided to drive by the Caribbean Club for herself. From the outside, it didn't impress, much to her disappointment. A sign on the door said it opened at six. It wasn't even five p.m. She peeked through the windows. It looked dark. Not because the lights were off, but the general mood was dark. The walls were plastered with posters and photos. It didn't look like the smoky, sexy place Bogart and Bacall had exchanged smoldering looks in.

Disappointed, tired, but still ravenous, Brenda decided to head back to the Casablanca Resort. She had to settle for a cold shrimp pasta salad from their small café. Exhausted, Brenda went back to her cottage. She slipped off her shoes, unpacked her pajamas and slipped under the bedspread. The sheets smelled like bleach. Brenda didn't even want to guess why housekeeping needed so much of it to keep them clean.

The sound of voices woke Brenda from her deep sleep. The slivers of sunlight coming through the blinds told her it was morning. She got up, still groggy, and stumbled to one of the windows. There was already a family out on the beach, two small toddlers building sandcastles with their bright plastic pails.

She searched around the room for an alarm clock or clock radio or anything with the time on it. There was nothing.

"This is taking it a bit too far," she mumbled to herself as she reached for her wristwatch. It was a little after eight. She knew the Keys touted the laid-back image, the "getting away from it all" mystique, but a clock here and there wouldn't be too much to ask for.

She dressed in a khaki pullover and navy cotton pants, plus slip-on shoes. After brushing her teeth, she swept her hair behind her ears and went in search of coffee and food. Her stomach was becoming vocal in its demand for something. She had passed out last night with only that shrimp salad for the whole day. She was famished.

Brenda drove to the Cracked Conch. It was a good choice. The place was a small wood building with a weathered look. She wanted to get an early start to Hilda Moran's, so she ordered a simple breakfast. One egg on toast and coffee. She was done by 9:30.

Doug Riddle, owner of Sunny Keys Tour and Dive Boat Charters, knew where to find Hilda's floating home. It was on the other side of Blackwater Sound in a secluded area of mostly mangrove forests. Brenda paid the deeply tanned young man and boarded an older, large, twin-engine boat with a bright blue canopy and the name *Mabrisa* painted in colorful script. She tried to push away the images of the last time she'd been in a boat. She rubbed at her left hand. The wound from Stewart Davis's bullet had left a tiny, lumpy scar there and a bigger one in her memory. No, she definitely did not want to be on this boat, but thank God that Doug was talkative and had a plethora of Key Largo jokes to keep her mind occupied.

The boat plowed the water at a leisurely speed and rounded one of the many small deserted islands off Key Largo. They veered right into a wide channel or "cut," as Doug called it. These were like fingers of water that cut into the land. The mangroves grew even thicker, extending farther into the water. Brenda got a claustrophobic feeling. The air was cooler out on the water. The scarf Brenda had opted for that morning whipped around her face.

They were deep into the channel when Brenda spotted what appeared to be houses up ahead. The boat slowed and as they got closer, Brenda saw that they were two homes, both two stories, side by side, just at the edge of the mangrove forest. They stood like two large sentinels, alone in the wilderness of green forest, aqua waters and blue skies.

It wasn't until the boat pulled up to the dock that she realized that these two-story homes were actually floating on the water. They were elaborate houseboats. She was surprised that this was where Hilda Moran lived. It was remote, to say the least, not exactly the most convenient location to conduct business.

Brenda waited for the *Mabrisa* to come to a stop and watched Doug tie the thick rope around the mooring pillars. She had rented the boat for one hour, so she didn't waste any time in disembarking. Doug said he'd be back promptly in one hour for her. She watched the *Mabrisa* slowly disappear with a sense of unease. She felt totally alone. What if Hilda wasn't home? It had been unprofessional to come out here without first calling. The only sound was the rippling of water around her. It was an eerie stillness.

She disliked walking down wood docks almost as much as she disliked being on the deck of a boat. The dock wound around the two houseboats. The address on the first one was Hilda Moran's. Unsure about which was the front part of the house, Brenda headed for the two French doors facing the water. The houseboats resembled modern wood-frame townhomes, with abundant windows on both floors. Stairs zigzagged from the bottom porch to the top veranda. There was hardly enough room for a small boat between the two houses.

Brenda walked up to the French doors, her PI card ready. She had her knuckle set to rap on the door, when both doors swung open.

"Come in, I've been expecting you," Hilda Moran said.

Chapter Two

Hilda Moran took Brenda's card, barely glanced at it and ushered her inside.

Brenda had seen Hilda only briefly at the autograph show in
Fort Lauderdale last December but hadn't forgotten how striking
she was. Hilda Moran was a tall, stylishly thin woman, probably in
her fifties, with elegant, European looks. Her olive skin comple-
mented the coiffed dark hair. She wore black pants and a matching
velvet top.

"Take a seat," Hilda said as she waved Brenda to a chair.

Brenda shivered. It was cold in the surprisingly spacious room.
Hilda's place was sparsely furnished, with a single couch, two
chairs and a computer that was set on a massive desk up against the
wall to the right. There were several closed doors Brenda assumed
led to other rooms. The houseboat/townhome appeared larger
from the outside than it actually was. Brenda sat down in one of
the tan leather chairs.

"I'm afraid I don't understand how you knew to expect a private investigator at your door." Brenda offered a slight smile.

Hilda lounged casually against the doorjamb, her arms crossed, studying her. Brenda guessed what was coming next. It was about time to seriously contemplate that plastic surgery again. She was tired of being a Princess Diana lookalike. She was certain it would prove to be detrimental one day in her PI profession. Looking like the departed Princess was not exactly a way to remain inconspicuous if one day she needed to blend into a crowd. It had been exciting and romantic once, especially when Tina was courting her and began calling her "Princess," but it was getting old.

"I would have remembered someone like you if we'd ever met." Hilda's voice was low, vibrant.

"We've never met," Brenda said, thankful Hilda hadn't mentioned her likeness to Princess Diana, but curious why she skirted her question. "I was at the autograph show this past December in Fort Lauderdale. Unfortunately, I was part of the crowd that watched the commotion between you and Clifford."

Hilda nodded slowly. "Ah, yes, that's where you met Clifford Satterly, I suppose. May I get you something to drink?"

Brenda shook her head. "No, thank you. The charter boat will be back for me in an hour. I'd like to ask you some questions."

Hilda sat down on the couch opposite Brenda and crossed her long legs in a smooth move. She reminded Brenda of a sleek cat.

"Very well, Brenda Strange, we can make this all business if you like." She set her dark gaze directly on Brenda. "The man is a lunatic. I mean it. He frightens me. Clifford's been calling and harassing me almost daily. He gloated about hiring you. That's why I knew you'd be knocking on my door eventually." She stopped and smiled. "And here you are."

"He just wants his manuscript back."

"I never got it, Brenda." Hilda sighed, clearly exasperated. "I mean, go ahead and investigate me all you want. I run a reputable autograph business and have never been in this kind of trouble before. I have appraised, bought and sold and authenticated everything from Abraham Lincoln handwritten speeches to a Stephen King inscription on a first edition. My reputation is spotless."

"There's always a first time."

Hilda shook her head. "My business is my livelihood. Having a good business reputation puts me above many of the other shady dealers out there." She waved a hand around the room. "The remaining square footage of my home is storage for my autograph inventory. I'm sure you noticed how cold it is in here. When you deal with paper in this Florida humidity, you've got to keep it from going brittle and disappearing in a number of years, so you keep your thermostat low. I am very dedicated. I suffer the cold of a meat locker and bear the expense it entails for my business."

Brenda didn't doubt her. Hilda Moran was certainly passionate about her profession, and that was exactly what could make her the perfect crook. Passion could lead to crime, and if the Malenko manuscript was as valuable as everyone thought, someone like Hilda might be motivated to do anything to get it.

"Maybe you should be checking with FedEx," Hilda continued. "They could have lost it. Misdelivered it. It could have been stolen. Perhaps it was never even mailed."

"One thing at a time, Hilda," Brenda said. "I'm checking every lead. I wanted to talk to you first." She pulled her notebook out of her bag as well as the paperwork from FedEx that Clifford had sent. "Were you home on . . ." She glanced briefly at the date on the receipt, then handed it to Hilda. "Were you here to receive mail on that date?"

Hilda looked closely at the copy, then waved it at Brenda. "I know I didn't sign for this. I didn't receive any package from Clifford. Maybe he lost it or someone else stole it and he's trying to pin it on me." She nearly flung the paper back at Brenda.

Brenda took the sheet, folded it carefully and placed it back in her bag. She focused a steely gaze back on Hilda. "What you're saying, then, is that someone put your signature on that receipt. Does anyone else have a key to your house? Friends? Family?"

"My nephew. Matt is the only other person who has a key."

"Does he come here without your knowledge?"

Hilda arched a perfect eyebrow. "There have been times." She stopped, obviously annoyed. "No, Matt wouldn't do that to me." She shook her head.

Brenda scribbled the nephew's name in her book. "Matt is your sister's, brother's . . . ?"

"He's my sister Heather's son."

"Heather Moran? Same last name?"

"Heather Ritter. She married and divorced."

"Does she live near here? How about the ex? Did he know anything about your business?"

"Heather and Matt live up in Homestead. Her ex-husband doesn't have money concerns. He's what you would call 'loaded' and living the sweet life with a young Hollywood wannabe in L.A."

Brenda wrote the names quickly in her book. "How old is Matt?"

"Sixteen. He's graduating this year." The smile on Hilda's face told Brenda that Matt was no ordinary nephew.

"How about his friends? Maybe he had impromptu gatherings while you were out?"

Hilda shook her head again. "No. He's a wonderful boy. Matt is selective. His close friends are few, all of them bookworms, if you will."

"Did he ever take any interest in your autograph business? Does he know the valuable inventory you store here?"

"Of course he knows what I do for a living, but we've never really talked in depth about it. He considers it an old person's hobby." Again Hilda smiled.

Okay, so Matt was an angel, but Brenda knew angels could fall from grace. "Can you tell me what exactly the Malenko manuscript is? That would help me out a great deal."

Visibly more relaxed, Hilda sat back on the couch. "I don't know as much about it as some others in the field, but I do know that the manuscript is one of a kind. It's the last written record left by Conrad Malenko, a Russian occultist who supposedly studied under the famous black magician Aleister Crowley."

Brenda paused in her writing. The name Conrad Malenko meant nothing to her, but she remembered coming across the Aleister Crowley name. She would have to dig deep in her memory to find him. "What makes this manuscript so special?"

"It's rumored to contain his teachings on black magic, complete with the ceremony for eternal life. Supposedly, it has some curse on it."

Brenda's ears perked up. "A curse? What kind of curse?"

Hilda waved a hand of dismissal. "Some silly legend or myth, I'm sure. If you really want to know about Conrad Malenko and the manuscript, you should talk to Arthur Clemens. You might have met him at the autograph show. He's the current president of Autographs International. He's made a devoted study of Malenko."

Brenda jotted the names Conrad Malenko and Arthur Clemens down in her book. She did remember Arthur Clemens from the autograph show. He'd impressed her with his impeccable style and penetrating eyes. She'd seen a capacity for malevolence in their gaze.

"Is Conrad Malenko still alive?"

Hilda shook her head. "No one really knows. He's a true mystery. He disappeared after the Second World War, leaving the manuscript behind."

Brenda was perplexed. Why would a man leave the formula for eternal life behind? "How did Clifford Satterly get hold of this manuscript?"

Hilda shot one eyebrow up. "He didn't tell you?"

"We haven't had long conversations." It was one of the things that made Brenda uncomfortable about the case. Clifford Satterly had been vague and elusive when it came to communicating. That would have to change if she was going to remain on the case.

"I only know what he told me, and that didn't sound right to me," Hilda said. "He said that after both his parents passed away, a key was left for him in the will. In the safety box of a North

England bank, he found the Malenko manuscript. He never told me why it was in a British bank and I never asked."

Brenda made a mental note to get more information from Clifford Satterly. She didn't think he was British. If he was, he was hiding his accent. "Hilda, how well do you know your neighbor?" Neighbors were oftentimes nosy. At least the ones Brenda remembered. The houseboat next door was close enough that whoever lived there could see a FedEx man come to Hilda's door. One good witness could prove Hilda Moran a liar.

Hilda laughed. "Forget it, you won't even get him to open the door. He's a writer. A retired electrician and living very well off his writing. I understand his Florida mysteries do quite well."

"Have you read any of his books?" Brenda asked.

Hilda shook her head and waved her off. "I have more work than I can fit into a twelve-hour day. I don't have time to read unless it has to do with the autograph business."

"What's his name?" Brenda asked.

"Jim Varley. He's sixty-something and your typical crotchety old man."

Brenda tore a plain sheet of paper from her notebook and handed it to Hilda with the pen. "Would you mind signing your name like you normally do?"

Hilda Moran took the paper hesitantly, looking at it as if it was laced with anthrax. "May I ask for what reason? I'm sure Clifford has sent you copies of anything he could get his hands on with my signature."

Brenda offered a tight smile. "Handwriting analysis. It's much better to work with an original sample than a copy. This will help you as well, you know. If you didn't sign for the manuscript, then someone forged your name. I need all the help I can get in finding who did."

Hilda hesitated only a moment before scribbling her name. She handed Brenda the paper and pen. "Will I see you at my door again? I travel extensively, Brenda. You took a chance coming out here. I might have been out."

Brenda put the signed paper in the notebook and put it back into the bag. "I don't like leaving messages on answering machines." She remembered FedEx. "There is one quick way to prove what you claim is true, Hilda. Come with me to the FedEx Central Hub in Miami. The driver who delivered this package might be able to remember who it was that signed."

Hilda contemplated her answer. "I can't do that today, Brenda. Will you be staying through tomorrow? I can meet you then."

"How do you get around, anyway?" Brenda asked.

Hilda couldn't help but laugh. "I have a boat behind the house, of course."

Since Brenda wasn't in a hurry to get back to Tampa and had reservations through Friday, she arranged to meet Hilda at 9 a.m. at the Casablanca Resort. Hilda gave Brenda a copy of the latest Autographs International newsletter that had the contact information for Arthur Clemens.

Brenda thanked her and was almost out the door but stopped.

"I'm just curious, Hilda. You don't have to answer, but why the remote location?"

Hilda gave her a sneaky grin. "You're right, Brenda, I don't have to answer you. It's a very long story. Sibling-related and professional reasons."

Hilda closed the door, leaving Brenda standing on the porch alone. Hilda hadn't exactly been gushing information yet seemed willing to cooperate to prove her innocence. Would she show up tomorrow morning? Brenda would have loved to search the place but suspected she would have come up empty-handed. If Hilda Moran had the Malenko manuscript, she was too smart to keep it lying around her house. But then again, what better place to hide a rare manuscript than in a climate-controlled, remote houseboat off the Florida Keys? And if someone had forged Hilda's name and stolen the manuscript, it was no doubt someone who knew the value of it. Heather or Matt Ritter might have known. She would have to question them.

She stood still for a moment and listened. There was only silence but for the whisper of the wind through the mangroves and the ripple of the water around her. From either Hilda's place or the neighboring houseboat, wind chimes tinkled. Beneath her, Brenda felt the whole structure move slightly with the current. She couldn't imagine ever being able to live in a house that wasn't firmly entrenched in dirt. Too much of her life felt like these floating houses, sitting precariously on unstable waters, doomed to sink at the smallest hole punched into their foundations.

According to her watch, she still had some time left before the charter boat came for her. She walked slowly to the edge of Hilda's porch and peered across at the other houseboat. She could jump it if she wanted to. There were no railings. Apparently, these houseboats weren't planned for neighborly get-togethers. There was no bridge or walkway between them either.

Brenda's curiosity about Hilda's neighbor was stronger than her fear of taking another dip into the water. Her last case had left her a bit water-shy. It was something she had to overcome if she intended to investigate, plus her curiosity was working overtime.

She crouched down, leaned back on one foot and jumped. She landed soundly on the porch of the other houseboat. If Jim Varley heard the commotion, he chose to ignore it, because not one of the blinds covering his many windows peeked open.

Brenda walked to the double doors exactly like Hilda's and knocked loud enough for Varley to hear. She waited but no one came to the door. There was no use trying to look through windows, because she wouldn't see a thing past the blinds. She knocked one more time, harder. She heard something or someone move inside. She was sure that somebody had come to the door and stopped. She could see a dark shadow through the bottom slit of the door that betrayed a body standing just on the other side.

"Hello? My name is Brenda Strange. I'm a private investigator. May I talk to you?"

No one opened the door. Brenda was distracted by the distant sound of a boat's engine. She turned to look out beyond the canal and spotted the charter boat speeding her way, the white crests parting before it.

As Brenda waited on the wooden dock, her cell phone chirped. She reached for it in her bag, careful not to drop it into the water. She'd already lost one that way.

"Am I glad I got you." It was Cubbie. "You better get back here pronto."

Brenda could tell she was munching on something. "What's wrong, Cubbie?"

"I don't know, sugar, but the FBI are here looking for you."

Brenda's stomach tightened. She let the words sink in as she watched the *Mabrisa* slide in and lean against the dock where she stood, the same sun tanned young man at the wheel. "What did they want? Did they say?"

"They wouldn't tell me anything other than if you weren't back in twenty-four hours, they'd come looking for you."

Brenda hadn't been in the game long, but she knew the FBI didn't bother with a small-time PI like her unless something big was up. What would the FBI want with her? "I'm leaving today. If they come back or call, just tell them that."

There went FedEx and Hilda Moran tomorrow, Brenda thought. She flipped the cell phone shut and stepped into the boat. As it sped off, she never bothered to look back at the two lonely houseboats disappearing behind her. Her head was filled with what waited for her at home. She wondered if it had to do with any of her past cases. She'd never had dealings with the FBI and didn't particularly relish the thought of the government looking into her affairs. She didn't know if it was the motion of the boat as it picked up speed on the water, but the butterflies in her stomach felt more like bumblebees.

Chapter Three

The guillotine blade fell with one quick thud and the woman's head tumbled into the bloody basket below. Her body jerked a few times but remained where it knelt, headless, the blood running like water down the wooden block, thickening the puddle already pooled there from the others before.

With a leather-gloved hand, the black-masked executioner wiped the guillotine blade free of the blood and bone bits that had stuck there, then kicked hard at the headless body. It toppled over as the hungry guillotine began its climb back up.

Another woman, faceless like the one before, mounted the steps of the platform and, without even glancing up at the sharp blade over her head, knelt before the wooden block. The executioner shoved her head into the groove of the block and raised one hand up in the air, ready to once again call the slicing blade down for another head. In one swift move, his hand moved down.

Brenda woke up startled, a stifled scream stuck in her throat. The room was cool, but she was drenched in sweat. She placed a hand over her chest to quiet her racing heart. Brushing strands of hair from her sticky face, she took a deep, calming breath.

What had brought on such a graphic and violent nightmare? She'd gotten to bed later than normal, exhausted after the long drive home from Key Largo. Driving conditions had been far from ideal, with long stretches of dark and brooding highway. But Brenda had stayed up deep into the night before without suffering such horrendous dreams.

She heard a demanding meow from the floor beside her and Butterscotch jumped atop the bed, strutting boldly to nuzzle against Brenda's side. The kitten's smooth fur under her hand relaxed her as Brenda took a deep breath and smiled.

"Hey, baby." She moved her face nose to nose with Butterscotch as he purred and kneaded the sheets. "Are you hungry, fella? Is your water dish empty or do you just want Mommy up?"

The kitten never failed to bring a smile to her face. Brenda knew how silly talking to a cat was, but to her, Butterscotch wasn't just a cat, he was a little person with fur. She knew most cat-lovers felt that way.

She glanced at the clock radio on the night table. It was five a.m. "Come on, baby." Brenda threw the comforter off, grabbed her chenille robe and wrapped it tight around her waist. "I may as well get up and keep you company. Can't sleep anyway." She flipped on the hall light.

Butterscotch followed her happily down the long upstairs hallway until Brenda reached the door to Tina's studio. She hadn't gone into that room since Susan Christie, the paranormal investigator from the San Diego Central Registry for Paranormal Studies, was here. The shadows that were spreading on the walls of Malfour, her home, had not gone away. They were multiplying. The dark stains had now appeared upstairs. The hallway was covered in shadows. But the most disturbing were located in Tina's studio. Susan Christie had discovered them while staying the week at Malfour last December.

Brenda opened the door carefully, not sure she wanted to proceed, yet drawn by a morbid curiosity. Butterscotch, suddenly abandoned, meowed his objection, twitched his tail and followed her into the room.

The image on the wall had grown, become more complete. She gasped, shocked at the image before her. The dark stains on the opposite wall had now merged and become what looked like a smudged drawing on the wall. In December, what had been a mere hint of a large head with bushy, flowing hair now had the distinct outline of a nose forming. And to Brenda, it looked decidedly feminine.

Unable to tear herself from the image on the wall, she looked more closely. It frightened her. What was this image going to become? What was Malfour trying to tell her? She remembered what Susan Christie had told her about the developing relationship with Malfour. Susan had strongly hinted that Malfour was seeking to become a conduit to the past, present or future through Brenda. She also suggested Brenda use her bond with the house to her advantage. To act as an oracle. The perfect bond between woman and house. The thought had frightened her at the time and she still hadn't changed her mind.

She needed to get out. She whirled around and shut the door quickly behind her, almost trapping Butterscotch inside. They both worked their way down to the kitchen, where Brenda fixed a strong cup of coffee and rewarded Butterscotch with extra kitty treats.

She had several hours before heading out to Strange Investigations. She knew she wouldn't be able to get back to sleep. Fearful that if she shut her eyes again, the same dreadful nightmare might return, Brenda sipped her coffee and decided to stay up with Butterscotch before taking a shower, dressing and leaving for the office.

❧

Brenda stopped at the bagel shop and picked up breakfast. Her mouth watered for a hot sesame seed bagel with cream cheese. She got Cubbie her favorite egg bagel. She didn't buy coffee because nobody made coffee better than Cubbie. Brenda would put her to work early to make a pot this morning.

When Brenda pulled into the Strange Investigations parking lot, there was a dark maroon late-model Ford parked in one of the spaces. What she didn't see was Cubbie's vintage VW Bug. The Ford was probably a Fed car. They all drove cars like that. Well, at least they did in the movies.

Brenda grabbed the bag of bagels and got out of her new Jaguar. She hated to admit it, but the brand-new Jag her dad had given her for her birthday was almost as much fun to drive as her old vintage '63 convertible.

By the time she got to the door of her office, a clean-cut white man in a suit and tie had emerged from the big Ford and was walking toward her. Even at a distance, she knew he was FBI by his looks. The badge dangling from the lapels of his blue suit only confirmed it.

Brenda plopped the bag of bagels on Cubbie's desk as the FBI man walked in behind her.

"Brenda Strange?" His voice was young.

Brenda turned to meet him. He couldn't have been more than twenty-five, with blond hair and green eyes. A weak chin revealed a protruding Adam's apple. He offered a quick smile and his hand.

"I'm Brenda Strange." She shook his hand. "I understand you were quite desperate to find me." Her empty stomach growled. Where was Cubbie?

The young FBI agent fished his ID wallet from inside his coat and offered it to Brenda. "I'm Special Agent Steven Selby, FBI foreign affairs with special attachment to the U.S. Marshals Service. I need a few moments of your time, Ms. Strange? There are some questions I'm hoping you can clear up for us."

Brenda looked over the shiny badge and photo ID carefully. The U.S. Marshals Service badge was a five-point star surrounded by a circle. It reminded her of an Old West badge. She handed the wallet back to him. She did know that the U.S. Marshals were part of the Department of Justice and that their jurisdiction was the U.S. mainland. "Foreign affairs? When did the Marshals extend their law into foreign countries?"

"There have been changes in all the agencies. Special ops Marshals have certain powers outside the U.S., Ms. Strange."

Brenda handed him the ID wallet back. "Why don't we step into my office?"

She motioned for him to follow her. She had all the time in the world, but not for spending it with an FBI agent. Glancing at the bag of bagels on the desk as she led Selby to her office, Brenda regretted the bagels would have to wait.

She opened the pebbled glass door, a throwback to the old *noir* private-eye movies, and wound her way behind the desk. She pointed to one of the retro aluminum chairs facing the desk. "Have a seat, Special Agent Selby."

He sat down, smoothing out his jacket, then crossed his legs. Eyes that reminded Brenda of the brilliant waters off the Keys looked steadily at her. He might have been young, but there was no lack of confidence in his eyes.

"Do you know Clifford Satterly?" he asked.

Brenda was surprised to hear the name. "He's a client."

"Can you tell me why he hired you?"

"I'm surprised at your question. Surely the FBI is familiar with client confidentiality."

"Ms. Strange, Clifford Satterly was brutally murdered. The Barcelona police found him in his car where, apparently, he'd been living. They turned the case over to us since Mr. Satterly was an American citizen."

Brenda was shocked. It was hard to believe. She'd spoken to Clifford only days ago.

Selby stared at her. "Since he hired you, Ms. Strange, I am assuming you have information that should be turned over to the FBI." He paused. "You understand that's why I'm here. You no

25

longer have a client, Ms. Strange. We'll need all the pertinent papers regarding the case turned over to us. It might help with the investigation."

Brenda was still trying to make sense of what she was hearing. Her response jammed in her throat. She coughed to get the words out. "When did this happen? I mean, when did the Barcelona police find him?"

Special Agent Selby didn't move a muscle in his face. "Three days ago."

"I spoke to Clifford three days ago," she said. "How did you find me?" Brenda wasn't sure she was willing to just hand over her case. She wasn't thrilled with the FBI muscling in on her job. Kevin's agency had had unsatisfactory brushes with the Feds. Besides, she didn't particularly care for Selby.

"Your name, phone number and address were found on his body," he said. "We traced his calls from the phone card he was using. You were the last person he called." Selby let the words settle in the air. "When did Mr. Satterly hire you, Ms. Strange?"

"He hired me last December," Brenda said, almost to herself. "I received a check and paperwork pertaining to the case. I—" Brenda stopped, pushed back the painful memories of her mother's death. "My mother passed away and I couldn't take the case right away."

"What did you and Mr. Satterly talk about on Tuesday?"

"He was agitated. He sounded frightened." Brenda recalled the conversation or lack of one. "He wasn't exactly chatty." She remembered his last words especially. "He thought he was being followed."

Selby's eyebrow shot up. "Did he mention any names, locations?"

Brenda shook her head slowly. "Nothing. As I said, he wasn't talkative." And if he had been, she wasn't so sure she would tell.

Steven Selby uncrossed his legs. "I'll take all the paperwork Satterly gave you, Ms. Strange." He leaned forward.

Brenda started to object but cooled down enough to realize she no longer had a client she had to protect. She was out of a case. Yet the thought of handing something that was hers to the FBI stuck in her craw. Something didn't feel right. It was all too quick. Too pat. Besides, the case fascinated her. She'd grown possessive of it. *No case can replace your mother.* "No, that isn't it," she almost said aloud.

Special Agent Selby was eyeing her oddly. She grabbed her bag and took out the legal-sized envelope Clifford had mailed her with the copies. Selby took it, barely glancing at it.

"Does the FBI have any leads?" She wasn't going to let go so easily. It had been her case, damn it. "Any idea why Clifford was killed?"

"It's against regulations for me to discuss a case." He paused. "But you did cooperate. The report we got from our offices in Madrid is that we have a body but no head."

"A headless body?" Brenda didn't recognize the squeak that was her voice. "Someone cut off his head?"

"Decapitated. Smooth cut, too. The worst part is that we can't find it. It wasn't with the body and we've had teams out in a ten-mile radius looking for it. Nothing yet. The Spanish police are talking cults but we're not ready to go that route yet."

Brenda heard the front door open and close. Both she and Selby stood up almost simultaneously.

"Hey, boss lady, I'm sorry I'm late and I see you got breakfast yummies . . ." Cubbie stopped at the door to Brenda's office. She looked a little ruffled, with her corduroy Chicago Cubs baseball cap slightly askew, blue jacket halfway buttoned and black pants. She looked at Brenda then at Steven Selby. She smiled sheepishly. "I'm sorry, Brenda, I didn't know you had someone in your office." She backed off.

"Cubbie, this is Special Agent Steven Selby, with the FBI." Brenda nodded toward him.

" 'Yummies'?" Selby arched an eyebrow.

"We met yesterday." Cubbie blushed. "I told him how much I loved Fox Mulder on *X-Files*." She appeared frozen in awe.

Brenda stared at her in disbelief. Cubbie wasn't herself. She'd never seen her blush before.

"Cubbie," Brenda said as she got up, "why don't you stick those bagels I brought in the toaster oven. Agent Selby was just leaving."

Cubbie waved a chubby hand in the air. "Oh, sorry. Of course. Good to see you again, Special Agent Selby." She made a sound Brenda swore was a giggle and grabbed his hand, shaking it vigorously. Cubbie walked out smiling.

Selby didn't move. He slipped both his hands in his pockets. "Ms. Strange, I don't need to tell you that Clifford Satterly is now officially an FBI case." He offered something that bordered on a smirk. "We don't like interference from private investigators or private citizens. Just so there's no misunderstanding, you're out."

This guy had balls Brenda would have loved to grab and yank hard till it hurt. He was giving her attitude in her own office. She flashed him one of her bright Princess Di smiles. "And so are you, Special Agent Selby." She pointed to the door.

He took the envelope and walked out without another word.

"Damn, boss lady, you chased that FBI guy out of here in a hurry." Cubbie had rushed out, a plate of steaming bagels in hand, looking disappointed. "I wanted to touch him again."

"You'd probably get a deadly virus." Brenda grabbed her sesame bagel and took a bite. Cubbie had slathered it with cream cheese. "We lost the Clifford Satterly case," Brenda said.

"The crazy guy from Spain? I didn't like him anyway."

"Be careful you don't insult the dead." Brenda dusted sesame seeds from her jacket.

Cubbie's eyes opened wide. "He's dead?"

"Not just dead. Decapitated. They found the body but not the head." Brenda pushed back the ugly scenes gathering in her head. First the dream, then Clifford Satterly.

Cubbie raised her shoulders and shivered. "What a horrible thing. Do they know who did it?"

"Apparently they don't have a clue, assuming the FBI really is on the case."

"Huh? What are you talking about, honey?" Cubbie looked at her, confused.

Brenda took what was left of her bagel and sat down on the edge of Cubbie's desk. She thought of Cubbie's love of the TV show *The X-Files*. "Don't FBI agents travel in pairs?"

"Scully and Mulder did."

"I knew you'd say that, but do the real Feds do it too?" Maybe that was what bothered her. Selby didn't have a partner. "We've still got the originals of those papers Clifford sent, right?"

Cubbie put her bagel down on the plate. "You pay me big money to do a good job, sugar. I locked away the originals and made copies of everything." She stopped and eyed Brenda suspiciously. She shook her head. "Oh, no, you're not going to keep at this, are you?"

Brenda finished off her bagel. She wasn't going to just hand her case over to anyone, even the FBI. Her distrust of Steven Selby was still nagging at her. There were ways of verifying FBI agents. Good thing all she handed him were just copies. Let him do his own investigating.

"Cubbie, I'm a sucker for expanding my knowledge base. The Malenko manuscript intrigues me. The FBI can't stop me from pursuing a hobby, now can they? Besides, intimidation never works with me." She smiled and winked at her. "Hey, where's the coffee that goes with these bagels, anyway?"

Cubbie swirled around. "I'm on it, boss lady." She took off to the file room that doubled as a break room. Brenda watched her go, her mind already in motion. The beheading of a body was a highly unusual murder. Clifford Satterly was living in his car. He was frightened of something or someone. In the middle of the gruesome puzzle loomed the Malenko manuscript.

"By the way, Cubbie," she called loud enough for Cubbie to hear, "Steven Selby was no Fox Mulder."

Chapter Four

Brenda sat in bed, trying to juggle the PowerBook on one leg and Butterscotch on the other. It was late. She'd tossed and turned until she finally gave up the fight, made some coffee and decided to go surfing on the Net. Butterscotch wanted equal attention. He purred and rubbed against Brenda until finally settling down beside her. Brenda gave him a soft kitty treat. She'd had to brush too many crumbs off the bed with the crunchy kind of cat treats.

In the search box, she entered the words *Conrad Malenko*, *Malenko manuscript* and *occultists*. There were only two hits for *Conrad Malenko*, both of them general histories of modern occultists. Brenda did find Aleister Crowley. It finally dawned on her why his name rang a bell. He was the most famous and flamboyant of the modern occult masters and hero guru to many of the late sixties and seventies hard rock bands like Led Zeppelin.

Surprisingly, there were hundreds of sites devoted to Crowley, but little for Conrad Malenko and his manuscript. Brenda found this odd. Did the manuscript really exist? For that matter, was Conrad Malenko a real person? Of the two Web sites that she bookmarked as favorites, neither shed much light on the manuscript, instead glossing over it as a book Malenko worked on for most of his life but never completed. He may as well have fallen off the face of the earth. One item of interest she found was that Malenko was linked to Hitler's Nazi Germany. Apparently, Malenko took an active role in the Nazi plunder and hoarding of art treasures throughout Europe.

More reason to suspect the scarcity of information on Malenko. If he was connected to Hitler, there should have been more than just two Web sites with minor bios on Malenko. Were there no devoted historians with an interest in Conrad Malenko and the rare Malenko manuscript?

Brenda clicked on Amazon. There was one book on Conrad Malenko. She shifted the laptop, petted Butterscotch and waited with enthusiasm for the page to come up. Her anticipation was crushed. The only book was *Malenko and the Black Arts* by a Herman Weissman. Unfortunately, it was out of print and not even available in Amazon's OP inventory. She could search other out-of-print booksellers or eBay, but she needed the information now.

She signed off, shut down the laptop and decided to hit the library in the morning. There might be something there.

"Come on, baby, you need to give Mommy space to sleep." She hugged the white-and-caramel-colored kitten and gently placed him at the foot of her bed. When she turned to fluff up her pillow, Carlotta sat on the antique chair beside the bed. It was Carlotta's favorite chair. Brenda had missed her favorite ghost. Both Carlotta and Angelique had been staying away since Susan Christie completed her investigations last Christmas. Things had gotten a bit out of whack.

"You are sad, Brenda." Carlotta's golden hair fell in curls down her beautiful 1920s-era gown. Both Carlotta and Angelique had been brutally slain and buried in Malfour House.

After Brenda and Tina moved into Malfour, Brenda began to experience the pain that still lingered in its walls. Carlotta and Angelique helped her solve their murder and bring the peace the two ghosts had yearned for. The bond that Brenda had forged with them kept Carlotta and Angelique in Malfour, more as grateful companions than frightening spirits.

Brenda shook her head. "Not sad, just tired." She stopped when she realized what Carlotta meant.

Brenda missed Tina madly. While Tina was home during the Christmas holidays, they had mended their relationship and fanned the fires toward something even deeper. Tina had bought Brenda the most stunning diamond ring. For a Christmas gift, Brenda had leased an art gallery storefront for Tina right on Howard Avenue, the major street that ran through Hyde Park, Tampa's trendy neighborhood. Brenda craved Tina's body next to her. Even though Tina had accepted a job at South Tampa University and would be home by late May or June, Brenda still suffered moments of depression.

She smiled at Carlotta. "I guess I can't keep anything from you ghosts."

If Carlotta blushed, there was no way of knowing. Her complexion was a waxy gray, not quite solid yet not transparent.

Brenda noticed a shadow creep into Carlotta's normally gray face. "You're sad too, Carlotta?" Brenda didn't know what to ask a ghost.

Carlotta rose from the chair like a wisp of smoke rising from a dying fire. She came to stand beside Brenda's bed. Butterscotch raised his head, stretched it as far as Brenda thought a cat could, took a sniff, then curled back into the comforter.

"Tina will be with you soon. Living here," Carlotta said.

She didn't elaborate.

"What's all this about?"

"What need will you have for us?" The ghost closed her eyes. Was she crying? Brenda was getting concerned. Carlotta had been acting irrationally ever since Susan Christie's visit. "What need will you have of me?" Carlotta's voice was almost a whisper, her gray-blue eyes staring into Brenda's.

Brenda wanted to touch her but knew she couldn't. "Carlotta, you know how I feel about this. Both you and Angelique know that as long as Malfour is my home, it's yours as well."

Carlotta shook her head of golden-gray hair. "But Tina—"

"Tina will understand. She's not the same. She's changed."

Brenda had to believe that. It hadn't been a picture of bliss when they first moved in and Brenda started talking to ghosts. Tina had freaked out and then walked out. But she came back, more willing to open up to the world Brenda was now a part of. A world Tina couldn't see, smell or touch. She would understand. She had to. "Carlotta, don't worry. Tell Angelique not to worry."

Carlotta smiled a wistful smile and evaporated. Brenda fluffed up her pillow and settled down under the comforter. It was four a.m.

"Great, that's all I need. A jealous ghost," she said to herself.

The John F. Germany library was located on Ashley Street, right off the Interstate exit into downtown Tampa. Brenda had been there for close to an hour this Saturday morning. She'd had to fight slippery streets from the drizzling rain that still fell outside. The lack of sleep was taking its toll on her. The puffy circles under her eyes had grown darker and she was having trouble focusing. At least she was thankful that not many had ventured out in the bad weather. Brenda had the library almost all to herself.

Despite being Tampa's main library, it didn't have a copy of *Malenko and the Black Arts*. None of the libraries in the surrounding counties had a copy. It came up as either lost or not available, whatever that meant. Surely, somewhere in the United States, a library had this book.

She walked up to the information desk where two well-dressed women sat, surrounded by computers and books.

"I was wondering if you might get this book for me through the

Inter Library Loan system?" Brenda handed one of the women the card on which she'd written the book's name, author and call number. Brenda noticed the name tag on the woman's blouse. Sue Chuey was short with shoulder-length graying brown hair and bright blue-green eyes. She entered the information into the computer, waited a few seconds, then frowned.

"I'm sorry, it doesn't appear in our statewide data bank. Let me check out our national library files." She offered a smile for Brenda. "We also have access to university libraries. I'll check those as well." The woman went back to her keyboard.

Brenda watched Sue Chuey work her fingers deftly over the keyboard. After what seemed like forever, the librarian frowned again, her eyebrows pinched together. She shook her head.

"This is very perplexing." She looked up at Brenda. "I'm afraid we can't get this book at all." She kept shaking her head. "I apologize. If you like, we can still try putting in a request, but . . ."

"Is it just not out there or are the copies checked out?"

"According to the state and national databases, copies of the book just never came back, for one reason or another, and the books were never replaced."

Apparently, *Malenko and the Black Arts* was as elusive as the Malenko manuscript. It was obvious Brenda wasn't going to get a copy of the book through traditional outlets. She thanked Sue, the librarian, took the card with the information on the book and left.

When she got home, she decided to give eBay a try. She wasn't going to get her hands on a copy of the book right away, so why not check out the auction Web site. Brenda entered searches for *Conrad Malenko, Herman Weissman* and *Malenko and the Black Arts*. She came up empty just as the Net search had.

Malenko and the Black Arts had mysteriously disappeared, just as Conrad Malenko had.

Chapter Five

It had been a spur-of-the-moment decision. Living spontaneously was not something Brenda did often. She liked to check her options and facts and proceed from there.

But she hopped on the Continental commuter flight Saturday afternoon on impulse after hitting the brick wall with the Malenko biography. During the forty-five-minute plane trip from Tampa to Miami/Dade airport, she'd had a chance to mull over what dragged her back to Key Largo and Hilda Moran. Susan Christie had challenged her to reach deeper into her psychic powers and open up to the possibility that her house, Malfour House, was trying to tell her something. Brenda had come to the conclusion that it wasn't the actual thought of having a direct link to Malfour that frightened her, but of what she might find within herself.

The dream the other night had been vivid. Violent. Faceless women were being inexplicably beheaded. In Tina's workroom at Malfour, the image of a woman's head was taking shape on the wall. With Clifford Satterly's gruesome beheading, Brenda was beginning to wonder if there might be some connection to all of these events.

There was unfinished business with Hilda Moran, business Brenda felt was part of the puzzle. She rented a car at the airport and headed out to U.S. Highway 1 and the glistening waters of the Florida Keys. Too bad she never wanted to go into those waters again. While admitting that the Florida coastline, with its beaches and water, was breathtaking, she opted to keep her Yankee complexion away from the sun.

The drive from Miami to Largo was a breeze. She certainly hadn't wanted to attempt the long haul all the way from Tampa in a car again. Once in Key Largo, she sought out Sunny Keys Tour and Dive Boat Charters. The same young man, Doug, with the white smile and tanned face, greeted her as if she were an old friend. She paid him, boarded the *Mabrisa* and was on her way back to Hilda Moran's floating houseboat.

As the boat pulled leisurely out of the marina and veered toward Blackwater Sound, Brenda decided now might be a good time to dial Hilda. If Hilda wasn't home, she could give Jim Varley another try. She almost expected Hilda's answering machine to pick up again. She was surprised when a man answered.

"Detective Garbano."

Brenda's insides turned to ice. Something was wrong. She could count her heartbeats as they thumped hard. Yes, something was very wrong.

Brenda cleared her throat. "I'm looking for Hilda Moran." She prayed she'd dialed the wrong number.

There was hesitation on the other end. She imagined a hurried team of detectives plugging into the phone and listening.

"May I ask who's calling?" His voice was suspicious.

"This is Brenda Strange. I saw Hilda several days ago about a manuscript." She wasn't going to give this Detective Garbano any more information until she knew what was going on.

"I'm sorry, Ms. Strange. Hilda Moran was murdered. Are you a business associate? A friend?"

"I'm a private investigator." Brenda barely whispered the words as she felt the bile come up in her throat and burn. Pictures soaked in blood rammed into her mind. She shook her head hard to get them out.

The *Mabrisa* began to make its sharp turn to the right as it approached the canal where Hilda Moran once lived. The air, suddenly cold and harsh with salt, sent tiny flecks of white foam into the boat as the twin engines droned smoothly. But Brenda heard nothing around her. There was only the dull, sickening thud of a guillotine echoing in her brain.

"Ms. Strange? Hello?"

The voice seemed to come from far away but it was in her ear. Brenda held the cell phone rigid in her hand. She'd gone into some kind of daze. She shook her head again. She strained to catch sight of the twin houseboats ahead.

"I'm on my way to Hilda Moran's house now." Brenda managed to sound as calm as possible.

The detective was clearly irritated. "I'm sorry, that's not permitted. Private investigator or not, you can't come. This is an active criminal investigation in progress."

"I'll see you in a few minutes." She flipped the phone shut as a chaotic scene came into focus before her. There were two large boats with the words *Monroe County Sheriff's Office* in big black letters on the side surrounding the two houseboats. Blue and red lights bounced above the boats.

Doug let out a low whistle. "Wow, so that's where all those Monroe police boats were racing to. Something big is going on there." He maneuvered the *Mabrisa* toward the dock, dodging the bigger police boats. He managed to slip in alongside Hilda Moran's houseboat and set the engine on idle. "You sure you want to get out?" He looked at Brenda with an arched eyebrow.

Brenda took hold of her handbag and hoisted herself out of the *Mabrisa*. "Wait for me." She approached the French doors with some apprehension. She'd been here only days ago. Hilda Moran had been alive with passion for her autographs. She couldn't be dead. Brenda wanted to believe that it was someone else dead inside. The police had made a mistake.

Before she even opened the door, a plainclothes police officer stopped her. He'd come from around the other side of the house. "I'm sorry, ma'am. You can't go in there. This is a crime scene. We're taping it up now. Are you a relative?" His partner appeared behind him, a roll of yellow police tape in his hand. He moved slowly, running the tape against the wall of the house.

Brenda dug out her private investigator license as she cast her eye to the badges dangling from the officer's belt. She wasn't really sure what good a PI card did her in this situation, but she was about to find out.

The young cop gave it a quick look, and then shook his head. "I'm sorry. I still can't let you in."

The door flew open and a short, dark-haired man rushed outside, running his hand through the gray on his temple. He wasn't in uniform but wore khaki Dockers and a long-sleeve blue shirt, badge dangling from his belt. From inside, voices thick in argument reached Brenda's ears. The short man looked at her.

"Who the hell are you?" He cast an irritated look back at the younger detective. "I told you no one was to break the crime scene."

The young detective objected. "But Detective Garbano—"

"I'm afraid I didn't give him much of a choice," Brenda interrupted. "Detective Garbano, I'm Brenda Strange." She offered her hand. "We talked on the phone. Hilda Moran was a suspect in one of my cases."

Garbano's mood didn't soften. He didn't take Brenda's hand. Instead he scowled. "Well, you can scratch her off your list now. She won't be of any more help to you." His voice was exhausted. He looked at Brenda closely. "What did you suspect Ms. Moran of?"

Brenda couldn't take her eyes off the French double doors. There was no need to ask for a sneak peek at the murder scene. She already knew what the sickening site looked, smelled and tasted like. The image was burning the insides of her head. Why was she being blasted with the scenes and sounds of death? If a scream could wipe the scent of blood from her mind, she would howl like a wolf.

The detective's voice broke the trance. "Ms. Strange? You need to answer some questions for me here."

"She was accused of stealing a rare manuscript."

"Accused? By whom?"

"It doesn't matter. He's dead now." Brenda wanted to soak in her bathtub to wash the sensation of blood off her body.

Detective Garbano didn't look happy. "It might very much matter." His head pointed to the doors. "We've got a pretty messy scene in there and if your investigation is linked to this, we might get a break."

Brenda locked eyes with him. "Was she beheaded?" She hoped her voice didn't quiver.

Garbano flinched, looked away and then back at Brenda. He started to furrow his brow but stopped. "How did you know? You either explain to me where you got that information or tell me you're psychic. Either one doesn't sit well with me." He shook his head and ran a hand through his hair again. "Listen, I've seen what some sick sons of bitches have done, but this . . ." He paused. "The nephew and sister found her."

Brenda shivered. An image jolted her as if she'd been hit by a lightning bolt. It was of a headless Hilda Moran sprawled across her couch, one arm dangling to the floor. The blood was everywhere, splattered and pooled. Brenda composed herself as best she could and focused on the detective's inquiring stare.

Yes, I'm a freaky psychic. But I don't want it! Brenda wanted to shriek into his face, hoping that if she screamed loud enough or maybe pounded her head into a hard brick wall, the images would stop coming.

Someone opened Hilda Moran's door. Another plainclothes detective poked his head out. "Hey, Garbano, the techs have some questions about the body."

39

Brenda cleared her thoughts. "Detective, my client was murdered in the same way. He was beheaded. They haven't found his head." She hesitated.

"We don't have a head either," Garbano answered. "Where was your client murdered?"

Brenda shook her head. "I know what you're thinking, but this isn't a serial killer. My client was killed in Barcelona, Spain."

"When? Days ago? Hours ago?" His eyes shone with intensity.

Brenda could imagine what he was thinking. It was very possible that whoever had killed Clifford Satterly could have stepped onto an airplane and not long afterward, murdered Hilda Moran. But who and why?

"Detective, I'll be happy to give you all the information I have if it will help." As Garbano moved toward the doors, Brenda grabbed his arm. "Where are Hilda's sister and nephew now?"

Garbano looked hesitantly at her, then nodded toward the other houseboat. "We couldn't let them stay here. They're with the old writer next door." He moved away but stopped again and pointed a finger at Brenda. "Don't leave Key Largo until we can talk. Leave your phone number and the address where you're staying with one of my detectives." He disappeared inside.

Brenda stood with the other two detectives, one of them still setting up the tape around the houseboat. The cool air helped her calm down as she got her nerves under control.

With Doug still waiting in the *Mabrisa*, Brenda decided to talk to Heather and Matt Ritter. Hilda Moran had mentioned her sister and the nephew she had obviously idolized. They were both here under one roof. An opportunity like this might not come along again, and something deep in Brenda was screaming for answers.

The police had set up an aluminum ramp connecting both houseboats. Brenda was glad she wouldn't have to make that jump again. She walked across carefully and approached the two front doors. She knocked and, this time, someone opened the door.

Chapter Six

The man who stood facing Brenda and holding the door as if to keep from falling was in his sixties. Dark circles sagged under clear blue eyes, and he sported a stringy gray goatee and bushy, unruly hair. It had to be Varley.

"Who the hell are you?" He clearly wasn't pleased to see Brenda.

"Mr. Varley?" she asked.

"So you know who I am and I don't care who you are. If you're not with the police, this door is slamming in your face."

Brenda certainly didn't want to get off on the wrong footing in this situation, but Varley's attitude was tiring and rude. She handed him one of her business cards, but he refused to take it.

"I have enough paper in this house without your card."

"I'm a private investigator," Brenda said, hoping the exasperation didn't show in her face. "I was here several days ago to speak with Hilda. I knocked on your door."

Varley narrowed his eyes and scanned Brenda from head to toe. "The police say it was okay to be here?"

Brenda nodded slowly. "Detective Garbano didn't object. I just want to speak with Heather and Matt."

In one quick move, Varley flung the door open wide. "Well, come on in. But I'll warn you now, don't expect me to tell you anything. It wasn't my idea for these people to be in my house. The police forced them on me."

Brenda wondered what could cause a human being to become so bitter and angry. Maybe the solitude and lonely profession of writing had gotten to him?

Varley didn't move from the doorway. Brenda had to inch by him. He smelled of disinfectant soap.

"They're upstairs in one of the bedrooms." He followed her into a room jammed with old furniture, books and nautical décor. The walls were paneled and the seascape paintings crowding the walls made the room seem even more claustrophobic. What a difference from Hilda Moran's sparsely decorated houseboat.

Brenda's feet sank into multicolored shag carpet that could have been installed in the seventies.

Varley pointed up toward a staircase tucked behind a wall that separated the kitchen and dining room. Varley must have gotten a good deal on the carpeting because even the stairs were covered with it. She went up the short, cramped stairwell and, as soon as she reached the second-floor landing, heard a male voice talking in a quick, borderline-hysterical manner.

There were two rooms upstairs. The voice came from the first room to her left. She stood at the doorway and found a twin bed in a room darkened with more paneling and somber drapes. A small dresser and two nightstands completed the furnishings. A woman and young man sat on the bed, the young man leaning over, his face hidden in his hands.

The woman who stroked his back stood up when she saw Brenda in the doorway. She looked at her with the hunger of anticipation on her face. "Is there more news? Have they found out what happened? Who did it?" She brushed off a strand of her shoulder-length hair that Brenda could best describe as the color of gingersnap cookies.

Brenda shook her head. "I'm sorry, I'm not with the police." She handed the woman her business card. The woman read it carefully, then cast her eyes over every inch of Brenda's body. Was she looking for a badge? She kept the card.

"Detective Garbano said it was okay to talk to you and Matt," Brenda said. "You are Heather Ritter, Hilda's sister?"

"I'm Heather Ritter." She looked at Brenda suspiciously. "Are you working on the case with the police?"

Matt got up and joined them. His eyes were a deep blue and shaped like perfect almonds. They were moist with tears. "Mom, what's going on?"

"Matt?" Brenda asked although she knew, and offered her hand. "I'm Brenda Strange. I spoke to your aunt several days ago. I was coming back to see her today. I'm very sorry about what happened. Detective Garbano says you found her."

This was part of the job that Brenda disliked. Pummeling family members with precise questions regarding a deceased loved one was insensitive and ghoulish. She rationalized it away by making herself believe that it was necessary if justice was to be had. It was the only way to help her find the person or persons responsible.

Matt Ritter was one of those tall, gangly boys who still had to grow into their bones. He didn't meet Brenda's eyes.

"I found her," he whispered.

"Did she know you were coming?" Brenda asked, then turned to Heather Ritter. "Were you with your son when he found Hilda?"

Heather met Brenda's gaze. "I was supposed to drop Matt and pick him back up in a couple of hours. He and Hilda were filling out some papers." She finished, but it sounded to Brenda like there was more to it.

"You own a boat then?"

43

"I do. In case you haven't noticed, it's the only way to get here."

"Does Matt drive that boat on his own?"

"Matt isn't old enough to drive the boat." Heather cast a defensive look at her.

Brenda turned back to Matt. "Matt, do you mind telling me what you and your aunt had planned?"

He shrugged, shifted his weight from one foot to the other and looked at his mother. "What difference does it make now?" When he looked back at Brenda, his eyes were filled with tears. She regretted asking the question.

"Look, if you aren't with the police, why are you asking all these questions?" Heather Ritter had no tears in her eyes.

Brenda would have to back off. She was no longer on the case and the police might object to her badgering their suspects. She dug out another one of her cards. "Matt, your aunt spoke of you fondly and I'm sorry this happened. I was talking to your aunt about a manuscript, the Malenko manuscript. If you can remember anything about it, please call me." She handed the card to Matt, who took it and stared blankly at it.

He finally shook his head. "I don't recall her talking about anything like that, but yeah, I can call if—"

"Matt, honey, why don't you wash up and we'll go back down and see if Detective Garbano can let us go home," Heather interrupted, rushing her son out of the room and turning to face Brenda. "Unless you have police authorization to talk to my son, I don't want you contacting us. I don't have to tell you what kind of a shock this has been to Matt, to us, and we'll have all we can handle with the police."

Heather Ritter was hostile and frightened. It was apparent by the way she wouldn't meet Brenda's gaze.

"I'm really sorry about your sister, Mrs. Ritter. I hope the police do catch who did this." Brenda thought it best to exit.

She didn't see Detective Garbano outside, so she left one of her cards with the address of the Casablanca Resort written on the back with one of the younger detectives still taping up Hilda's houseboat.

Brenda went back to Doug and the *Mabrisa* with more questions than answers. If Heather and Matt Ritter knew anything about the Malenko manuscript, they weren't talking. If there was one positive thing from her meeting with Heather and Matt, it was that Matt had pocketed her card.

Detective Garbano didn't show up but called two hours after Brenda got back to the resort. He couldn't say much about the case but assured her that he would be contacting her within the next couple of days.

Brenda had breakfast at the Cracked Conch the next morning before heading back to Tampa. She debated whether to have a big breakfast or something light. After a few minutes of indecision, she decided on an English muffin, lightly buttered with strawberry jam, and coffee.

When the muffin was placed in front of her, it had already been buttered and the jam liberally applied. She couldn't eat it. Her stomach suddenly felt heavy. Bloated. She downed the coffee in a couple of hot gulps, left a two-dollar tip and left.

The strawberry jam had looked like blood.

Chapter Seven

Brenda intended to put the disturbing events of the Satterly case behind her at least for a couple of days. Early Monday morning, she got up, called Cubbie and told her she'd be late, then headed out to Tina's new gallery. Buying a small gallery for her lover had been a big move for Brenda. After the breakdown of their relationship after moving into Malfour, things were mending. No bridges were burned and Tina was moving to Tampa with a new teaching job at South Tampa University. Their love was as strong as ever and this past Christmas had been the perfect time to get the space for her.

Tina wouldn't have to beg gallery owners anymore to take on her sculptures. She could have her own openings and keep all the profits from her sales. It had been one of Tina's dreams. The gallery was located in a strip of Howard Avenue that was a hopping location and a popular nightspot packed with eccentric shops, bookstores and white-tablecloth restaurants. And only ten blocks from Strange Investigations.

Brenda and Tina had discussed names for the gallery and finally decided on Marchanti Gallery of Fine Sculpture. Brenda promised Tina she'd get everything done so that when Tina came home for spring break, the gallery would be ready for her to move in and decorate.

Brenda parked in the space directly in front of the gallery. The painters she'd hired were inside, busy putting Tina's chosen color on the walls. Navaho White.

Brenda was pleased to see the carpeting down and most of the painting done. Ed Banners, who had overseen the restoration at Malfour House, had recommended the painters.

The painter in charge told Brenda they could wrap it up by the end of the day if she'd okay a couple of extra hours of overtime. Brenda wanted it done, so she agreed and left. Tomorrow, the custom-made sign would be going up outside the gallery. She'd have to make time tomorrow to be there.

She headed back to Strange Investigations, but not before stopping at Teddies in the Park. Brenda thought she should stop in and speak to Felice about her Zodiac Bears. Brenda's line of miniature bears for each sign of the zodiac had been a hit. Teddies in the Park was the exclusive shop locally for the Zodiac Bears, but Felice, the owner, had successfully marketed the line nationally. She'd been bugging Brenda about an article for one of the teddy bear magazines. Brenda could barely keep up with the orders she had already. If she appeared in a magazine, she might have to get someone else to help her make the bears, and she was unsure how she felt about that.

Making miniature bears had been the one thing that had kept her sane in the months following her near-death experience last year. Sewing together teddy bears had become almost a spiritual journey. Each little bear brought back the warm feelings she had needed to connect with her inner being. Bear making took Brenda back to her childhood. Back to Timmy before he became a ghost.

Felice's shop was a delight, with teddy bears of every shape and size peeking out from shelves, corners and tabletops.

"Brenda, what a pleasant surprise." Felice stepped out from

behind one of her counters and walked up to give Brenda a big hug. There was no one else in the store.

"I wanted to apologize for not getting with you about the bears sooner. I've been trying to catch up on a case I had put off after my mother passed away."

Felice put her hand on Brenda's shoulder. "Maybe you should take some time off instead of trying to catch up."

Brenda smiled. She was perfectly aware that Felice's concern was genuine, but she didn't know what Brenda needed. "I just came by to let you know that I got your order sheet and I'm starting work on the Pisces bear this week."

"Pisces? What happened to Aquarius?" Felice cocked her head in thought. "Isn't that the next zodiac sign after Capricorn?"

"You're right, it is, but I wanted to skip Aquarius. Just can't seem to come up with a good enough image for the bear, and I have this fabulous idea for the Pisces one." Brenda didn't think they had to keep up with the zodiac signs. Collectors would buy the bears no matter what month they were released. She patted Felice on the back and smiled. "Trust me, when you see this new one, you'll forget all about Aquarius."

Later that evening, after feeding Butterscotch, Brenda couldn't resist calling Tina. The gallery was coming along well and she wanted to share the news with her lover. They hadn't spoken for over a week. Tina had gotten stuck with a class of exchange students and was spending extra time with them in class and then taking the load of work home. Brenda had promised to wait at least one week before disturbing her with phone calls. She missed Tina more than she thought possible and couldn't wait for her to finish the semester at the Newark Art Institute and come home.

They were discussing the limited parking at the gallery when Brenda's cell phone went off. Normally, the cell meant business or an emergency. Although she mostly wanted to ignore it, she felt compelled to answer. It might be her father. Or Detective Garbano.

After smacking kisses into the phone for Tina, Brenda said good-bye and reached for the cell phone. She didn't recognize the number on the display. Brenda pressed the green "on" button.

"This is Brenda Strange."

"Hello, Ms. Strange?" The female voice paused. "It's Heather Ritter. I didn't know who else to call."

The name immediately brought back the memory of death and blood. "Heather, is everything okay?"

Heather whimpered. "No. No, it isn't. I'm afraid for both my son's life and my own."

"Try to calm down. Take a deep breath. Tell me what's wrong." Brenda opened the drawer of her desk, pulled out a notepad and sat down on the leather sofa. "Heather?"

"The police . . . they . . . uh, called me the morning after Hilda—" She stopped.

"Did they find who did it?" Brenda hoped against hope that Detective Garbano had found a lead.

"No. They found Jim Varley floating in the water near his houseboat. They said it was a homicide and that's all they would tell me."

Brenda couldn't control the shivers that ran up her back. What possible motive could there be for Varley's murder? Was it connected to Hilda's death and the Malenko manuscript?

"Did Detective Garbano question you again?" Brenda asked.

Heather Ritter cleared her throat. "No, it wasn't Detective Garbano. There is no Detective Garbano in the Monroe County Sheriff's Office. I don't know who those men were. That's why I'm so freaking frightened. The police, the real Monroe County police, came to my house and questioned Matt and me." She was almost screaming. "I don't know if I can handle this. I'm so scared."

Brenda's thoughts were scrambling to make connections, to

make sense of what Heather had said. Brenda couldn't fight off the feeling that she was holding something back. Something big.

"Heather, I want you to do me a favor and take your time and tell me everything. What kind of questions did the police ask? Do they have any idea who those men at Hilda's houseboat were?"

"I need to hire you, Ms. Strange."

"You don't need a private investigator, Heather. Just cooperate with the police."

"No. You don't understand. I stole the manuscript. I stole that freaking manuscript."

Chapter Eight

"It wasn't supposed to turn out like this."

There was a surprise waiting for Brenda on Tuesday morning. Heather Ritter sat across from her at Strange Investigations. She shook her head and yanked another tissue from the square Kleenex box on her lap. Brenda had told her she'd call her when she came up with something that could help her.

"I mean, if I'd known Hilda would be murdered . . ." Heather bowed her head as tears spilled out from already red and swollen eyes. "I never in my life wanted my sister dead. Not that way."

Her shoulders quivered as she sobbed quietly.

Brenda couldn't stand to see women cry. "Let me get you some water." She got up and opened the office door. Cubbie and Matt were watching one of those reality courtroom shows. "Cubbie, can you bring some water, please."

Brenda closed the door gently and sat back behind her desk. Heather Ritter and her son could be in extreme danger. Brenda's

51

body was tingling with a sense that something decidedly wicked circled around this Malenko manuscript. So far, anyone who'd come into contact with it had ended up badly.

Despite the fact that Brenda very much wanted to be back on the case, she knew this was something for the police. Heather Ritter was in trouble with the law. Not only that, but she had information that might help them find who murdered Hilda Moran.

"Heather, I can't take your case. The Monroe County police could be looking for you as we speak. You broke the law the minute you forged Hilda's signature and stole the Malenko manuscript and now you're jeopardizing Matt's education by dragging him out of school. I take it you were the one who forged your sister's name?"

Heather blew her nose loudly and plucked another tissue from the box. She looked at Brenda with wet, defiant eyes. "Today is a teacher conference day at Homestead Senior High, so there's no school and yes, I forged her signature." She stopped and Brenda thought she was going to start crying again. She didn't. "That's why you have to help me. I'm scared out of my wits. I don't know who else to turn to."

Cubbie walked in balancing a tray with a large pitcher of water and two glasses. She set the tray on top of Brenda's desk.

"Thanks, Cubbie." Brenda offered a smile. Cubbie didn't linger. She closed the door behind her. Brenda poured half a cup of water and handed it to Heather, who took it in one swift move. "Heather, I'm here to help in whatever way I can. Even though I can't work for you, I feel I have a vested interest in finding out what happened to your sister." Brenda paused and watched as Heather downed the water in two gulps. "I'd like you to tell me exactly what happened that day. Take your time."

Heather put the empty cup down, inhaled deeply and sighed. "I'd gone to Hilda's to talk about Matt's college tuition. Matt wants to be a lawyer. My sister was going to pay for it all, college and then law school." Heather paused, looked at Brenda, then down at the ball of tissue in her hands. "We argued a lot about that."

"About what? Matt's going to law school or Hilda paying for it?"

Heather shook her head. "Hilda always acted like she was better than me. Her paying his tuition was just her way of showing off her money to Matt."

Brenda was beginning to see that Heather Ritter and Hilda Moran had a bitter sibling rivalry. "I can think of more worthy things to argue about."

"C'mon, how would you like it if your sister was trying to buy your son?" The venom was thick in her voice.

"You thought Hilda was trying to take Matt from you with her money?"

"Well, not literally. But she always lavished her attentions and money on him. He couldn't get enough of her."

"Is Matt your only son?"

"Well, yes."

"And Hilda's only nephew?"

"Yes." Heather sounded annoyed.

"Did Hilda have children?"

"No, she never married."

It sounded to Brenda like Hilda had formed an extremely close relationship with Matt Ritter to make up for the son she never had. "Don't you think Hilda might have genuinely loved your son as her own?"

Heather shot Brenda a startled look. She squared her shoulders. "Why are you asking all these personal questions? This isn't about Matt."

"Maybe not, Heather. I'm trying to help you out. The police are going to ask questions far more personal than these. You should be prepared to answer them." Brenda put both her hands on the desk and stared deeply at Heather. "Now, tell me why you were in your sister's town house."

"I wanted to talk to her, Ms. Strange, that's all. I love my son and I want him to accomplish his life's dream of practicing law, but I also want him to be proud of his mother. I figured I could talk Hilda into making me a loan for Matt's schooling. I would pay her back little by little. It sounded like a good idea."

"How did you get to Hilda's? Your own boat?"

"Of course. In case you didn't notice, it's the best way to get places in the Keys."

"Does Matt have access to the boat? Has he ever taken it without your knowledge?"

"He doesn't know how to drive the boat. I take him where he needs to go." There was irritation in her voice.

"Was Hilda home when you arrived at her place?"

"She wasn't there. I had Matt's key so I just went in and decided to wait for her. And then the FedEx man came to the door. I knew Hilda dealt in valuable antiques, so I signed for the package and took it home."

"It sounds like you two were in competition for Matt's affection. Maybe after you took the package, you decided to eliminate your rival?" Brenda let the words hang in the air.

Heather shook her head hard. "No. I never wanted harm to come to my sister. I admit I was very jealous of the relationship she and Matt had. They both spent lots of time together. Hilda had been there from the beginning. She watched Matt while he was growing up and I had to work to support the both of us. Then Hilda established her autograph business and bought the houseboat so she could work from home." Heather paused, her words fading. She wiped another tear from her eye. "Matt felt safe with Hilda."

"Safer than with you?"

"I didn't kill my sister." Heather slammed a fist on Brenda's desk.

Brenda couldn't stop now. She didn't always like this part of her job. Badgering people had been fun in a courtroom, but this was different. She was dealing with raw, unstaged emotions.

"Why did you forge your sister's name and steal the manu-script?"

Heather's rage softened. She slumped back into her chair and looked at Brenda with pleading eyes. "Hilda was going to pay for Matt's entire tuition. How do you think that made me feel? He thinks I'm a failure. I can't even afford to put him through college. I took the chance that package contained something that might be worth some money."

"And you hoped that by selling the manuscript, you'd have enough to pay for your own son's college?"

Heather whimpered. "It was stupid. I know." The tears flowed freely again down her cheeks. She shook her head. "Oh, my God, Hilda is dead because of me." She yanked out extra tissues and buried her face in her hands.

Brenda didn't need to ask Heather Ritter any more questions. Heather didn't kill her sister. And neither did Matt Ritter. Hilda's killers were far more dangerous and powerful. They were on the hunt for the Malenko manuscript and anyone who stood in their way met a horrible death.

Brenda poured Heather another glass of water. The important thing now was to make sure Heather, Matt and the manuscript got back safely to the Monroe County Sheriff's Office. "Heather, where is the manuscript now?"

"It's in the trunk of my car."

Brenda stood up. "I'm going to give you advice you shouldn't think twice about taking. You've got to head back to Homestead and go directly to the police. Have them contact the Monroe County police. Don't stop for anything or anyone on the highway. When you get there, call me and let me know everything is okay." She leaned down closer to Heather. "Do you understand me?"

Heather looked bewildered. Like a frightened rabbit. "Why do I need to leave so soon? What do you know? Have I been fol-lowed? Are we in danger?"

Brenda didn't have positive answers for Heather and she didn't think Heather would feel at ease if Brenda admitted all she was going on was a psychic warning and the pictures of bloodied, headless bodies crowding her mind.

"Listen, Heather, you've stolen something the police need to help them find your sister's killers. You need to turn the manuscript over to them. Besides, you'll be safer under police protection in Homestead."

Heather was shaking her head again. "But what if they're fake too?"

It took some convincing to get Heather Ritter out the door of Strange Investigations and on her way back to Homestead and the police. She appeared hesitant and afraid. It was no wonder, Brenda thought as she drove onto Swan Avenue on the way to Tina's gallery. The group of police imposters at Hilda's had already spooked Heather and she wasn't alone. Brenda felt uneasy about who Detective Garbano really was and what his interest was in Hilda Moran. Could it be the Malenko manuscript? And what if Garbano, or whoever he was, had killed Hilda?

Brenda pulled up to the gallery storefront, parked her 1963 Jag convertible and got out. The gallery was finished. The small blue canvas canopy that Brenda had special-ordered had been installed directly over the large gallery window. The name *Marchanti Gallery of Fine Sculpture* was painted in white on the canopy. They had done a good job.

Since she was here, Brenda decided to go inside and take a final walk through the gallery to make sure everything was cleaned up. For some reason, the empty gallery made Brenda feel lonely. It needed the life that only Tina could breathe into it with her stunning sculptures. Brenda needed her lover for different reasons than the sculptures.

Brenda took Bayshore Boulevard back to Malfour. Even though the smell of Tampa Bay at low tide was sometimes foul, she loved the beautiful drive by the bay.

It was after 5:30 and the sinking sun was painting the sky with purple, orange and blue. The air was crisp but not cold. There was no need for Brenda to put the top up on the vintage Jag, her pride and joy. She loved the fact that at least in Florida, she could drive with the top down for most of the year. The weather wasn't the enemy like it was in New Jersey.

As she drove the Jag smoothly through the curves of Bayshore, Brenda couldn't help but let her thoughts float back to Heather Ritter. Brenda anticipated her phone call from the Homestead Police station. Would the police want to speak with Brenda? She was intrigued by the case yet disturbed by some of the occurrences that had manifested themselves with it.

She couldn't blind herself to the recurring dreams of headless corpses and the persistent scent of blood. She remembered her first visit to Malfour House. The strong, acrid smell of burning wood had stung her nostrils. Neither Tina nor Cindy Taylor, the realtor who sold them the house, had smelled it. It took Brenda time before she discovered that she had somehow acquired a psychic sense of smell. She felt sure it was her near-death experience that had gifted her with extrasensory abilities.

Apparently, her psychic nose was at work again. But what did the smell of blood mean relating to her situation? Traditionally, the term symbolized the experience connected to predators in the hunt for prey. But how did that expression fit in with her dreams or the Malenko manuscript? Or was it something else? But what? Brenda was halfway convinced that it had something to do with the murder of Clifford Satterly and Hilda Moran. And the Malenko manuscript. But too many of the puzzle pieces were still missing.

As Brenda drove past the Gulfbreeze restaurant on the 22nd Causeway, she thought about stopping for blackened grouper. She didn't feel like fixing anything for dinner and she was hungry. But her indecisiveness cost her the grouper dinner. She sped past the Gulfbreeze, thinking of skipping supper entirely. Maybe a bowl of cereal would do the trick.

She turned at the entrance to the Tides of Palmetto. The bright aqua letters on the red brick sign still beckoned to the rich and influential community. One of the things that had charmed Brenda about the Tides was the isolation. A short two-lane bridge was the only access to the community. For extra security, you had to stop at a guardhouse. If you didn't live there or weren't expected by someone who did, you didn't get past the guards. And of course, there was Malfour House.

The house stood like a defiant antique among the cookie-cutter modern mansions of glass and plaster that made up the rest of the homes. Sea Breeze Lane was the first turn off the Tides Boulevard, the main road that wound through the Tides.

As Malfour House appeared over the mangrove and palm trees, Brenda smiled, filled with a sense of relief. She knew that once inside the walls of her home, she was always safe, forever welcomed.

It was dark inside Malfour. The sun had just sunk below the horizon, making the house inky with shadows. Brenda flicked the switch and 200 watts of recessed lighting bathed the foyer in soft illumination. But she could still see the shadows on the walls that refused to fade despite the lights. She stood defeated in the foyer, surrounded by black stains running through all the walls of her home. Shadows only she could see. Susan Christie had been vague on what they meant.

From what Brenda understood, they were some sort of link to her own psyche, a reflection of her inner powers. Too much mumbo jumbo, she thought. She preferred not to see the shadows. Not to smell the blood, but she'd come back from the grip of death with psychic awareness and was now stuck with this new "gift." Some gift. Too bad she couldn't return it for a refund.

She was halfway tempted to hire an exorcist to try and get rid of the shadows on the wall. If she could be assured her ghostly companions, Angelique and Carlotta, wouldn't be included in the exorcism, she would do it.

She sighed, wishing Angelique or Carlotta was there to greet her.

"Angelique? Carlotta?"

They either ignored her or were somewhere else wherever ghosts hung out. Instead, Butterscotch came pounding down the stairs and wove through Brenda's legs.

"Hey, baby. Are you hungry?" She kicked off her shoes at the foot of the stairs, filled Butterscotch's bowl with food and fixed herself a cold Belvedere vodka martini. She was getting low on olives and made a mental note to buy another jar.

It was 6:30 by the time she went through her day's mail and worked her way upstairs to her studio. She'd promised Felice at Teddies in the Park another Zodiac Bear. To Brenda, there was nothing more relaxing than sipping a martini, listening to her favorite music and working on her miniature bears.

She pulled down the roll of white suede, a box of miniature green sequins and her six-compartment Rubbermaid container crammed with upholstery needles, thread and bear supplies. Brenda had experimented with different materials to stuff her bears with and liked the plastic pellets best. It gave her bears a "weighted" effect. At the teddy bear show in Orlando last December, she discovered the most exquisite black eyes imported from Germany. She'd bought two boxes of them.

The Pisces bear was going to be a mermaid, the bottom part of the bear covered with green, glittering sequins. With a Sagittarius and Capricorn bear already sold out, Brenda purposely passed over the Aquarius bear. Brenda was an Aquarius herself, but that wasn't why she skipped it. She was stumped on what the Aquarian bear should be. The zodiac symbol for Aquarius was the water carrier, most often depicted as a woman pouring water from a jar. Tina had suggested a Chinese bear carrying two pots of water on its back with a cute little pointed straw hat.

Brenda laughed at Tina's idea and dismissed it, but unless she could come up with a better idea, the Aquarius Zodiac Bear might end up looking like Tina's bear.

Instead of one of her jazz CDs, Brenda plucked an Indigo Girls CD from the stereo cabinet in the studio. It was Tina's favorite group, one she kept urging Brenda to try. Tonight, she decided to do just that. The title of the CD was *Retrospect*. She punched in selection No. 16.

The harmony between Emily Saliers and Amy Ray was smooth and soothing. Brenda let it play. True, the sound was folksy, not usually her cup of tea, but it was Tina's music and tonight, Brenda needed to be close to Tina.

By the time Brenda had cut the fabric into individual pieces, the CD had ended and the martini glass had gone dry. And it was near 9 p.m. Where was Heather Ritter? She hadn't called. She and Matt had left around 2:30 that afternoon. If she'd listened to Brenda and hadn't stopped, she should have been in Homestead hours ago.

The shrill ringing that echoed through Malfour startled Brenda out of her mellow mood. It was the phone. Was it Heather calling from the police department? Brenda and Tina had both agreed to no phone in their studios. No phone, no disruptions.

Brenda ran to the bedroom.

"Hey, darling. Took a while to answer the phone. Everything okay?"

The mellow tone of her father's voice was soothing. She felt her shoulders sag and let out a sigh of joy. What she wanted most desperately was to reach across the phone lines and wrap her arms around her father.

"I just walked in the door, Dad. How are you?" When she'd left her father in Tarrytown, New York, in February, he'd seemed drained of energy. Although both Brenda and Tina had made most of the arrangements for her mother's funeral, Raymond Strange had looked very much a lost man. Tonight, his voice had energy to it.

"I'm fine, honey. Your Aunt Miriam and Uncle George have been here most of the week. I wish they'd leave." He laughed. Aunt Miriam and Uncle George were a handful. Brenda could imagine the hectic state her father's day-to-day life was with them as houseguests.

"You know they just have your best interests at heart. They don't want you to spend so much time alone."

"But I'm fine, sweetheart. Really."

Although Brenda thought otherwise, his vitality was apparent over the phone. He was going to be okay.

"Anyway, honey, I hope I didn't interrupt anything. I called because Gary Blanchette dropped by with a box your mother apparently left for you. It's got your name written in big letters."

Brenda's heart thumped hard and her ears went red hot. Gary Blanchette was her parents' attorney. Why had her mother left a box for her? Her relationship with her mother had been dysfunctional to say the least. Only illness and impending death had brought them closer. What was in the box?

"Why don't you go ahead and open it, Dad? You have my permission." She would much rather her father deal with it.

"Can't do that."

Brenda could almost picture her father shaking his head.

"Gary said your mother left specific instructions that only you were to open it," he said. "How about I mail it to you tomorrow, Wednesday, and overnight it? When you open it, you can call and tell me what's inside."

How could she refuse? Her mother had never mentioned a mysterious box to her. "Sure, Dad. Just mail it here to Malfour House."

Brenda had to admit that her curiosity was piqued. She was truly stumped as to what it was her mother had wanted only her to see.

Chapter Nine

After the conversation with her father, Brenda just couldn't concentrate on her Pisces bear. She put away her supplies and decided to call Mark Demby at the San Diego Register of Paranormal Studies. It was after six in California, but he usually worked late. Mark had been a godsend, knowledgeable in all things paranormal. Brenda wondered if his knowledge base extended to the occult. If he didn't know about Conrad Malenko, he might at least point her in the direction of someone who did.

"Conrad Malenko?" Mark paused. "Can't say I know much about him. He was some kind of occultist in the thirties, I think. If I remember the brief bio we have on file, he wrote what was supposedly a treatise for attaining immortality. Rumor had it that he put a curse on the manuscript. We don't have much ourselves. There is a book about him."

So Hilda had been telling the truth about the curse. With the unusual number of dead bodies now connected with the manuscript, the "curse" was something Brenda wanted to know more about. "Does anyone know about this curse?"

"Nope." Mark sighed. "It's just one of those rumors that seems to have taken on a life of its own through time."

"The bio is impossible to find," Brenda said. "Do you know anything about the publishing company or the author?"

"Well, it was published in nineteen-fifty. It's been out of print and unavailable a long time. The author never wrote another book. He just dropped out of sight." Mark paused. "Are you involved in another case, Brenda, or are you just getting into black magicians lately?"

Brenda smiled. She liked talking to Mark. He was a friend and associate. "Mark, I can't answer that."

"You already did. I won't pressure you, though. Listen, if I can be of any help whatsoever, don't hesitate to call."

Brenda hung up, still unsatisfied and antsy. It was 9:30. Heather Ritter's call was long overdue. She'd had ample time to arrive in Homestead. Not wanting to dwell on worst-case scenarios, Brenda decided to call Arthur Clemens. His name was connected with Conrad Malenko. Hilda had mentioned his interest in the Malenko manuscript. If anyone could help her, it would be Arthur Clemens.

She dug out the business card Hilda had given her and dialed the number. Brenda wasn't sure if it was a home or office, but it was worth a try. The address on the card was in Ft. Lauderdale, Florida.

He picked up on the first ring. "Arthur Clemens."

"Mr. Clemens, this is Brenda Strange. We met at an autograph show in Ft. Lauderdale in December. I was with Eddy Vandermast."

There was slight pause on the other end. "Brenda Strange, the private investigator."

Brenda imagined that sneer on his face. "I hope you don't mind my calling you. Hilda Moran gave me your card. She said you were an expert on Conrad Malenko and his manuscript."

He was quiet again. "I heard about Hilda. I can't even bear to watch television. It's all over the news. I am shocked and depressed that some monster could have done that to her." He paused. Brenda got the impression he was choosing his words carefully. "Hilda and I were friends and colleagues. I will be happy to help you if I can, but may I ask if you're investigating the disappearance of the Malenko manuscript?"

"I'm not investigating anything, Mr. Clemens. My interest in the Malenko manuscript and Conrad Malenko is purely personal." The partial truth was better than a complete lie.

"Ah, I see. Conrad Malenko has captured your imagination. I can understand."

"Then you'll answer my questions?"

"But of course, Ms. Strange. I have spent considerable time researching the greatest black magician of our lifetime."

Brenda wanted to waste no time. "Tell me about the Malenko manuscript and the curse."

Clemens laughed, but he didn't sound jovial. "Well, I think you know something about the manuscript already, since you spoke with Hilda. Most scholars believe that Malenko had the secret to eternal life and that he wrote it, longhand, in the form of a book, with the entire occult ritual, except that he left out the last page and kept it hidden from everyone, even his closest friends. The story is that Malenko had to make a hasty retreat from Germany when the Allies invaded, leaving the book behind minus the last page. Without that missing page, no magician on earth could complete the ritual for immortality. And for good measure, he put a curse on the manuscript."

It sounded like a cruel joke to Brenda. "What about the curse?" She was beginning to sound like one of those old, broken windup dolls repeating the same programmed question.

Clemens sighed into the phone. "It isn't something any scholar of Conrad Malenko believes"—he paused—"but the curse warns that a horrible death will befall any and all who attempt to hold or own the manuscript other than Conrad Malenko. And of course, no one has been able to prove or disprove the curse because the real manuscript has never been found."

"Horrible death" stuck in Brenda's brain. Hilda and Clifford had died horrible deaths. But if she was going to buy the curse theory, it would mean Hilda had had the manuscript and lied about it.

"Mr. Clemens, do you think Hilda and Clifford died horrible deaths?" Brenda hoped she didn't sound too much like a private investigator on a case.

He laughed. "If you mean do I think the curse had anything to do with their deaths? No. I recently found out about poor Clifford. We were not close friends, but I'm sorry about his death."

"So you don't believe there is a curse?"

"No, and I don't think you should either." He laughed again.

Brenda believed that both Hilda Moran's and Clifford Satterly's deaths were brutal and somewhow connected to the Malenko manuscript. If not a curse, then someone, cold-blooded enough to butcher innocent people, believed the missing manuscript was the real thing and was apparently willing to continue killing to get it.

"As a scholar of Malenko, aren't you the least bit curious as to why both Hilda and Clifford were killed? Supposedly they both possessed the manuscript at some point. Someone out there thinks it's the real thing. Do you?"

Arthur Clemens didn't laugh this time. "I've been faced with so many fraudulent copies and dealers insisting they had the real Malenko manuscript that I've approached all claims with suspicion. I would very much like to find the manuscript that Clifford claimed was the real one, but until the manuscript is actually placed in my hands for authentication, I can't afford to let myself get caught up in this sort of speculation."

His calculated answers made her wonder. "You know, Mr. Clemens—"

"Arthur, please," Clemens interrupted.

"Arthur," Brenda continued, "from my own research, I've learned that there is precious little on Conrad Malenko. How can you or anyone else authenticate anything—in this instance, the manuscript—with so little existing historical material or facts? There's only one biography on him."

"You pose a good question, Brenda. *Malenko and the Black Arts* is one of those satisfying biographies where the author had personal information, making it a complete bio in all senses of the word. The book has photographs of the actual manuscript and reproductions of some of Malenko's personal letters. It's an invaluable work in authenticating any real Malenko documents."

Brenda sat up on the edge of the bed. "You have a copy of Herman Weissman's Malenko bio?" *Please say yes*, she repeated to herself silently.

"No real Conrad Malenko scholar would be without *Malenko and the Black Arts* in his library."

Bingo. Someone actually had the book! She should have called Arthur Clemens first. "Arthur, what other documents are in the book? Where are they now?"

"Ahh, that is something no one knows. Herman Weissman disappeared. I'm afraid Conrad Malenko remains as much a mystery in death as he was in life. I think that's what makes historians more interested in people like Malenko. We like to dig deep in the hope of finding that elusive document or letter, much like an archeologist consumed with unearthing what was thought long lost to civilization"—he paused—"or a detective trying to find those elusive clues that are not apparent to the less trained."

Brenda rolled her eyes. Arthur Clemens was long-winded and full of himself. Her first impression of him hadn't softened. He was a snob, but at least he'd been moderately helpful. "What are the chances I might borrow *Malenko and the Black Arts*?" She figured her chances were slim to none for that happening, but she'd been surprised often enough in life.

Again, Arthur Clemens laughed. "Brenda, you know how hard it is to find a copy of that book. I don't even let it out of my personal library."

"I can buy the book. I'm willing to pay the price. Do you know where I might find a copy of it?" Brenda wasn't kidding. Now more than ever, she felt the information in this book could be useful in cracking the mystery of Conrad Malenko and the manuscript. Indirectly, it might shed some light on why Hilda and Clifford had been murdered. Besides, she had the money.

"Well, there is one authenticator who might possibly be able to help you, but I can't promise anything, Brenda. It's been some time since I corresponded with him."

Excited yet frustrated, Brenda disconnected with Arthur Clemens. Talk of curses brought back the bittersweet memory of her and Tina's move to Malfour and the curse put on them and their house. Detective work, courage and persistence put an end to that curse, but Brenda was uneasy about the Malenko manuscript and the deaths of Hilda and Clifford. Was there truth and power to the curse surrounding the manuscript? And if so, was Heather Ritter on the short list now? Brenda's thoughts were moving like blazing bullets through her head. Heather hadn't called and that worried her. She considered calling the Homestead or Monroe police but decided tomorrow morning would be best. Maybe Heather and Matt stopped somewhere on their way to the police. Even though she had warned Heather against stopping, Brenda also understood human nature. They had to eat. Use the restroom.

There was a powerful danger connected with the Malenko manuscript. She resisted believing it could be a curse, but two people with supposed ownership of the real Malenko manuscript had been murdered. She didn't want Heather or Matt to be next.

It was late, but Brenda decided to treat herself to a glass of Merlot before bedtime. Sitting on the smooth vanilla-colored leather couch in the Malfour library, she tucked her feet beneath her and took long swallows of the full-bodied red wine. She wondered how soon Arthur Clemens would get back to her. Would he call at all?

She finished the wine, turned down the lights in Malfour and went upstairs to bed. With Butterscotch curled up against her side, Brenda couldn't fight off the drowsy effects of the Merlot. She drifted easily into sleep. And there, the nightmare waited, hungry and eager to tear into her dreams.

Tina mounted the steps of the guillotine stage, striding purposefully to the block of stained wood in the center. Behind the black mask, the executioner smiled.

Like a mindless zombie, Tina dropped to her knees and rested her head on the blood-drenched block. Above her, the guillotine blade hung high in the air, waiting to sever bone, tendon and head. Tina's head.

The black-garbed executioner yanked hard at the guillotine lever, releasing the killing blade. It screamed in the foul air as it came down. Tina waited, unflinching.

Brenda jerked up in bed, awake and gasping for air, a scream jammed in her throat. Her fists clenched the sheets around her. She was drenched in sweat yet couldn't stop shivering.

After taking a few deep breaths, Brenda calmed down. Her breathing returned to normal and her heartbeats weren't pounding in her ears. She wiped the sweat from her face with the back of her hand and noticed Carlotta sitting on the wing chair beside the bed. Her favorite spot.

"Carlotta. How long have been there?"

Carlotta looked sad. She shook her head. "Long enough to know you were having that nightmare again. It looked like you were fighting with your own pillow."

Brenda smiled. Carlotta was a frequent visitor, almost watching over Brenda. After the séance Susan Christie did last Christmas, Brenda became aware that Carlotta had developed a crush on her. A bit confused, since Brenda didn't really know what ghosts felt or couldn't feel, she decided not to bring the subject up with Carlotta.

"Yes, it was a nightmare. The same one." Brenda stopped, swept her hair back from her face and eyed Carlotta suspiciously. "Wait a minute, I don't remember telling you about my recurring nightmare."

The ethereal form of Carlotta shimmered and shook. A giggle, Brenda presumed. "As Angelique and I continue to live here with you, we are discovering new powers."

"I'm almost afraid to ask," Brenda said.

"Sometimes, we can read your thoughts. Feel what you feel."

Brenda's jaw dropped. "Now wait a minute, that can be embarrassing, not to mention an intrusion into my privacy."

Carlotta seemed hurt. "Please don't worry. It isn't something I would do to hurt or embarrass you."

"Well, how do I know when you're up there in my brain?" Brenda had to admit that part of her found it amusing.

"Angelique and I are experiencing new things. We only want to help in any way we can. I—Angelique and I, that is, are very excited to experience these new things."

Brenda couldn't really be angry with Carlotta. In fact, maybe she could help. "Carlotta, since you know about my nightmare, can you tell me what it means?"

Carlotta shook her head slowly. "It's very frightening. Obviously, it involves Tina and I believe it portends harm to her."

Oh, great, that's all Brenda needed to know. Now she had to worry about what might or might not happen to Tina. She shook her head to clear the nasty thoughts collecting there like a pool of rancid sewer water and sunk back down on her pillow.

The clock radio said six a.m. It was just starting to get light outside. Although her body was screaming for more rest, Brenda decided to get up and head to Strange Investigations early. Maybe she could beat Cubbie there for a change.

She brushed her teeth, then dressed in a tan corduroy jacket shirt, black pants and boots. And with Butterscotch weaving between her ankles, she headed downstairs for a cup of coffee.

Staying active, she believed, was the best medicine against

obsessing over her nightmares and Malenko. She also wanted to call the Homestead police this morning. Something was wrong. There was a reason why Heather Ritter hadn't called.

Brenda had just taken a swallow of coffee when her cell phone chirped. She looked at the information display. It was Cubbie. Brenda smiled.

"Cubbie, do I need to stay up all night to beat you to work?"

"Boss lady, you better rush over here pronto." Cubbie sounded serious. Too serious.

"What's wrong? Are you okay?"

"Oh, I'm fine, sugar, but there's a big FedEx package on the front doorstep of the office with a big ol' note written in hand by Heather Ritter. Looks like she just plopped it at our doorstep. If it's what I think it is, I don't want to touch it."

Brenda thought her heart stopped for a moment. Could it be the Malenko manuscript? But why had Heather left it and where was she now?

"Don't touch anything, Cubbie. I'll be right over." She left the coffee on the kitchen table, made sure Butterscotch had plenty of food and water and ran out the door.

Chapter Ten

Dear Ms. Strange,

I wish I could fix what I did wrong and bring my sister back, but I can't. I only know I have to continue to protect and provide for my son. I'll live with the guilt for Hilda's death all my life.

I'm not going to the police. If they want to question me, I'll tell them everything, but I won't continue carrying this manuscript around one minute longer. I believe my sister died because there are evil people after this manuscript. I'm leaving it with you. You can turn it over to the police. I've written my phone number below. I'll wait for the authorities to call.

Heather Ritter

Heather Ritter's letter was written on hotel stationery. The Tahitian Inn was a newly renovated hotel on South Dale Mabry. Heather had taped her letter neatly on top of the FedEx box.

When Brenda arrived at Strange Investigations, she'd found Cubbie waiting inside the front door and the FedEx box propped up next to the door. Brenda had taken the box to her office to read the letter. Cubbie, uncharacteristically quiet, busied herself making coffee.

Brenda placed the letter beside the box and turned her attention to the object responsible for two deaths, possibly three. The address label, smudged and barely readable, showed Hilda Moran's name and address. There was a return address from Clifford Satterly in Spain. An insurance sticker was pasted on the upper right-hand corner. Brenda wondered how much he had insured it for. What price had he put on such a reportedly priceless document?

The box had been opened. Heather had indeed been very curious. She'd taken a look at the manuscript. Probably hadn't understood at all what it was she'd stolen. The manuscript inside beckoned to Brenda. What did it look like? Conrad Malenko had written it by hand. Was it in Russian, his native language? All she had to do was dig the manuscript out of the box and all those questions would be answered.

Brenda took a deep breath and pulled open the flap. Cubbie, coffeepot in one hand and two mugs in the other, stopped in mid-stride at the door.

"Don't touch it, Brenda!" Cubbie had a look of horror on her face.

"No bats or demons are going to fly out of the box, Cubbie," Brenda joked, shaking her head. "Pour us some coffee and pull up a seat."

"I'll pour the coffee but I ain't stayin'."

"Cubbie, what's come over you? I've never seen you behave like this." Brenda eyed her suspiciously.

Cubbie poured a full mug of the strong coffee for Brenda. "Look, sugar, I grew up with a deep respect for the powers of good and evil." She pointed to the FedEx box. "That thing in there is pure evil. It's already killed people. I don't want any part of it and neither should you. I'll be at my desk if you need me."

She took the coffeepot and her mug and rushed out. Brenda couldn't help but wonder if Cubbie's fear of the Malenko manuscript was so far-fetched. Had Jim Varley also been murdered because of his connection with Hilda Moran and Heather Ritter? Had the murderers in search of the manuscript thought Jim Varley knew something?

Brenda grabbed the box and without further hesitation pulled the manuscript out. The first thing that struck her was the condition of the pages. The paper had yellowed and the top page was stained with brown splotches. The other was the strong, elegant handwriting. It wasn't English. From her foreign language studies, Brenda recognized it as Russian, one she hadn't excelled in. Thankfully, the pages weren't torn or otherwise abused. Obviously, the manuscript had been stored and well taken care of.

Two leather cords tied at the top and bottom left side held the pages together. They could have been red at one time. Her curiosity running at mach speed, nothing could keep her from flipping through the pages. The handwriting was neat throughout. At the bottom of each page was a marking, presumably a page number. In her estimate, the Malenko manuscript appeared to be about a hundred or so pages. Some of them contained esoteric emblems and diagrams, the one recurring theme being the inverted Star of David. That emblem Brenda recognized. It was frequently used by black magicians and Satanists. Could the drawings be part of the fabled Malenko ritual of eternal life?

She was admittedly swept up in the allure of the manuscript. Was this unreadable stack of faded and stained papers what Hilda Moran and Clifford Satterly were murdered for? And by whom? The "why" part of the question was by far the more frightening. Brenda knew she had to contact the Homestead Police Department immediately. The manuscript would soon be out of her hands. Was she willing to part with it? She could make a copy for herself. The police didn't have to know. It would be a shame not to have this piece of diabolical history translated. Mark Demby could profit immensely if she turned over the complete Malenko manuscript to the Register for translation. Brenda couldn't let the nagging, building little voice of doubt stop her. What if the same horrendous fate befell Mark Demby?

Did she believe the horrible curse would strike her down? Not really. She wasn't that superstitious. What scared her more was the reality that very powerful, dangerous and sadistic people wanted the book and were willing to do whatever it took to get it. On the other hand, bad guys with guns she could handle. Well, maybe one guy with a gun.

Brenda had already made up her mind. Her office copier was a small HP PC printer/copier. It would take too long to copy the entire manuscript, and considering Cubbie's aversion to it, Brenda didn't think it wise to copy it at Strange Investigations. Cubbie would probably go into cardiac arrest if she knew Brenda was keeping a copy of the book for herself. Kinko's would be quicker and inexpensive.

She slipped the manuscript back into the FedEx box, grabbed her oversized bag and left her office. Cubbie was sitting at her desk, the television tuned in to *Wheel of Fortune*, its big wheel spinning and people screaming.

"Cubbie, I probably won't be back today. If you want to take the rest of the day off with pay, you can."

Cubbie shifted her attention from the TV to Brenda, gaze settling on the box under Brenda's arm. "You're getting rid of that, sugar, right? Did you call the police?"

There was no reason to lie to Cubbie. Brenda had had her fill of half lies and conniving in her law practice. "As soon as I make a copy."

The day turned dark, with thick purple thunderclouds crowding the gray skies, and a blustery wind kicked up. The temperature was dipping. Brenda had made the copy at Kinko's and before heading back to Malfour decided to call the Monroe County police from her car. They would be interested in the manuscript and in Heather's story. She talked to a Detective Reccio, who informed her that all the Keys were under their jurisdiction and that he was indeed interested in the manuscript and in getting the real story from Heather. He was dispatching two plainclothes detectives from Key Largo to Tampa and to expect them in roughly six hours or so. He also suggested she set aside a couple of hours for questioning. They'd have lots of them.

Brenda headed back to Malfour, hoping to beat the downpour that was coming. By the time Brenda turned off the 22nd Causeway onto the Tides of Palmetto entrance and stopped at the guardhouse, big fat raindrops were exploding on her windshield. It was just after three p.m., but you couldn't tell. The sky was dark iron.

Tony Cutcheon stuck his head out of the guardhouse door. He had his orange raincoat and hat on.

"Afternoon, Ms. Strange." He smiled and tipped his hat. Ever since he'd helped Brenda when she and Tina had first moved into Malfour, Tony was tripping over himself to be of service again. He was one of those young, tough-looking guys who believe they have all the answers.

Brenda flashed him her resident card. If you didn't live in the Tides or have a good reason to be there, the guardhouse was as far as you got. He barely looked at it.

"Careful on the bridge, Ms. Strange. We had it closed for a couple of hours today for the big moving rig. Appears you've got a new neighbor. Some big European exec is moving into the Davis house."

Brenda had known the Davis home was up for sale but didn't think it would sell that quickly. They were asking an astronomical price for it.

"Did you get to meet him?"

Tony shook his head. "Nah. A big black limo pulled up and the chauffeur was the only one that opened the window to show the resident card. I verified it and off they went."

"What's his name?"

Tony bent down and put both hands on Brenda's door. "Brad Smith. Maybe you should go and introduce yourself?"

"Thanks, Tony." Brenda was in no mood to play the welcome wagon. After what she and Tina went through with Stewart and Joan Davis, she wasn't feeling particularly neighborly. Brenda drove onto the narrow two-lane bridge, glancing down at the bay waters below. The increasing rain made tiny ripples in the brackish water.

As she approached her turnoff on Sea Breeze Court, she had to make a quick stop to avoid hitting the black town car that pulled out in front of her. Brenda gripped the wheel of the new Jag hard as she watched the limo disappear down Tide Boulevard. Only Malfour House lay at the end of Sea Breeze Court. What had the limo been doing down her street? Were they lost? Was it the new neighbor taking a ride down his new neighborhood—or worse, looking to pay her the dreaded neighborly visit? She hoped it wasn't the latter, but her PI senses told her to file the black town car and her new neighbor in her "might be important later" mental file.

Malfour House appeared like a shadowy, pale ghost behind the curtain of gray rain that continued to fall. Brenda didn't have an umbrella in the car or her bag, so the only way she knew to keep the FedEx box with the original Malenko manuscript in it and the Kinko's bag with her copy dry was to tuck everything under her jacket. She wouldn't mind getting soaked.

Once safely inside, she shivered as she stood in the foyer, her hair and clothes dripping. Desperate to get out of the wet clothes and into the warm embrace of a vodka martini by a quiet fire, she rushed upstairs, dumped the soaked clothes, slipped into a long flannel robe and fixed a strong martini with the last of her olives. She'd have plenty of time to get into dry clothes before the detectives showed up.

After plopping several logs in the library fireplace, she settled down with her copy of the Malenko manuscript. Tomorrow, she would try to locate a Russian translator. Some of the local universities would be a start.

With her martini in one hand and Butterscotch beside her on the couch, Brenda tucked her legs beneath her and settled deeper into the leather couch. Outside, the rumble of thunder echoed; some of the windows rattled in apprehension. Brenda began to flip the pages, looking intently at the ones with the drawings. None of it was in English, but the artwork and symbols were universal. In the arcane world of the occult, a true adept would be able to decipher all of the images. Unfortunately, she was neither an occultist nor a student of the black arts.

But even with her limited understanding and exposure to black magic, she was well acquainted with the inverted Star of David.

A loud clap of thunder shook the house again and lightning flashed angrily in the sky. Brenda nearly jumped out of her robe. Butterscotch bolted from the couch and ran for cover somewhere. She could almost feel the electricity crackling against the walls of Malfour. The sound of the rain against the windows intensified. She wondered if the detectives traveling from Key Largo would have to stop for the bad weather. She hoped for their sake that the storm would blow over before then.

Brenda knew it had to be her imagination, but the shadows crowding the walls at Malfour seemed to shift and change. She called out for Butterscotch, suddenly needing the warmth of another living thing beside her.

"C'mon, Butterscotch. It's just the lightning, baby."

The small kitten peered nervously from underneath the wing chair across from her. His frightened eyes made her smile.

She patted the leather seat next to her. "C'mon, baby boy, come back to Mommy."

Butterscotch couldn't resist her call and bravely scooted out from beneath the chair and back onto the couch, purring and rubbing against her.

She kissed the top of the kitten's head. "I'll keep you safe, Butterscotch."

With Butterscotch safely curled beside her, Brenda returned to the page with the first of the handdrawn images. This inverted pentagram was different, yet one she also was familiar with. Her law firm in Jersey had handled a case where a couple had been accused of satanic worship and the kidnapping of children for sacrifices. Some of the evidence the police had confiscated from the couple's home turned out to be satanic books on occult practices. One of them had been a large, black book with a silver inverted pentagram and the seated figure of a bare-breasted woman with the head and legs of a goat, hand raised in some sort of occult signal.

The Baphomet Goat. That was the image that now lay on Brenda's lap. Conrad Malenko had obviously been dabbling in the satanic arts. The Baphomet Goat had connections to the evil and darkest aspects of magic and ritual. The couple from Jersey had claimed their religion was a legitimate and benign one. Brenda wondered if Conrad Malenko practiced the same kind of "benign magic." Or was there something more sinister in the appearance of the pentagram and the goat?

Another bright streak of lightning flashed outside. She glanced out the window and dropped the manuscript she was holding. There was someone standing at the far end of her yard, next to the wooden bench at the edge of the water.

Startled, she approached the floor-to-ceiling window and, through the heavy wall of rain, noticed that the figure wore a black trench coat and black slouch hat. Both the coat and hat were dripping wet but whoever it was just stood there, staring back at her. He—or she—was too far away for Brenda to see a face. The image was ominous and disturbing. It couldn't be the police. They were hours away. And Tony at the guardhouse hadn't called advising of any visitors.

Without further thought, she rushed out of the library and up the stairs, almost tripping on her long robe. Whoever was out there, she didn't have a good feeling about it. There was something sinister about the figure.

She reached her bedroom, pulled out the PK Walther from her

drawer and turned to the window. The bedroom was directly above the library. She pressed her nose against cold, moist glass and looked down at the yard below. The stranger was gone. High on the second floor, she could survey her entire yard. There was no one there. The rain had changed direction and was now streaking at an angle toward her, the thick drops bursting in front of her face. She took another moment to scan the backyard. Nothing.

Gun at her side, Brenda ran back down the stairs, her heart keeping pace with her frantic steps. She rushed to one of the windows in the front foyer. Was there a car parked up front? Was the mysterious figure someone who'd gotten lost?

Her front driveway was empty; only a collection of small rain puddles dotted her front yard. Brenda went to every window on the first floor and saw nothing. Had it been her imagination? No, someone had been out there. Maybe it was time to call the guardhouse after all. Tony answered in one ring.

"Tony, this is Brenda Strange. Did anyone come in after me?"

"Well, yes, ma'am. You must be psychic. I was just going to pick up the phone and dial you. An FBI agent by the name of Steven Selby is here. He says you two know each other and that he's here on official business regarding a manuscript. He said you'd know what he was talking about." He paused. "Is everything okay? Do I let him through?"

"Everything is fine. Thank you. Pass him through." She hung up. What did Steven Selby want and how did he know how to find her? Did he know she had the manuscript? She was about to rush back upstairs to get dressed when Carlotta whispered in her ear.

"The evil man is gone."

Evil and *man* were two words Brenda didn't like hearing lumped together. She glanced around the foyer for her ghostly companion, who was nowhere to be seen.

"Carlotta, what do you mean, 'evil'?"

"Ancient as the hills," Angelique chimed in.

"Be serious, please," Brenda pleaded into empty air. "He really spooked me. What was he doing on my property?"

"He's shielded, Brenda," Carlotta said. "There is a dark veil he is hiding behind. And Angelique was right. He smells of age." She paused. "And evil."

Great. This didn't make Brenda feel any better. She'd just about had it with evil men trying to intrude into her life. Could the Malenko manuscript be related to the mysterious stranger?

The thought seeped through her innards like a slow poison.

As if she'd spoken aloud, Angelique answered her. "It's the book. It radiates the same evil as that old man out there."

Another lightning strike hit, followed by thunder that almost drowned out the ringing of the doorbell.

She approached the front door with a tinge of apprehension. Peering out one of the two long windows bordering the door, she saw a deep blue Chrysler sedan. It looked new. Brenda angled herself against the window to see Steven Selby staring back at her, a tight little smile on his wet face.

Brenda quickly tucked the Walther PPK into her robe pocket and opened the door.

Chapter Eleven

"Ms. Strange, we met at your office." He extended his hand. "Steven Selby. FBI." He went to yank his ID wallet from his dripping wet raincoat.

Brenda stopped him. "I know who you are. How did you find me?"

His face showed surprise. "It's really wet. May I come in?"

Brenda hadn't been expecting him and she didn't like that he was alone. "I don't usually allow strangers in my home."

Selby dropped his hands in exasperation. "I've been working with Detective Reccio from Monroe County." He paused and made a sweeping gesture. "As you can see, the weather isn't exactly ideal for traveling. I was here in Tampa and offered to come for the Malenko manuscript. They're pretty bogged down with flooded roads in South Florida right now."

Okay, so Selby knew Detective Reccio's name, but she still didn't feel comfortable letting him in her home. He stared at her, his blond hair dark with dripping rain.

He reached inside his raincoat. "Okay, I see you need some reassurance." He pulled out a cell phone and handed it to Brenda. "Go ahead, call Detective Reccio. I'll even dial for you."

Brenda snatched the phone from Selby's hand. She'd rather do the dialing herself. Just to be sure.

"It's number five on the phone," Selby said.

Brenda held the number five down on the phone. Detective Reccio answered on the first ring. They were indeed flooded in South Florida. He apologized for not being able to send his detectives and verified that FBI Agent Steven Selby had been working on the case with them. He also apologized for not calling her and letting her know of the change in plans. It was safe for Selby to take the manuscript. Arrangements had been made for him to bring it back to the Monroe County Sheriff's Office in Key Largo.

Convinced, Brenda said good-bye and handed the phone back to the drenched Selby. Grudgingly, she opened the door wide and ushered him into the foyer of Malfour House. Ignoring the doormat, he was making a puddle on her hardwood flooring.

"Let me take that wet raincoat from you." She was stuck with him for a while. He would want to question her on how she came to have the FedEx box and the elusive manuscript.

Selby peeled the tan raincoat off and handed it to her. She took it to the kitchen and laid it over the edge of a chair. Rushing back to Selby, she found him eyeing his surroundings.

"You've got a beautiful home, Ms. Strange." He smiled, turning his green eyes on her. Brenda didn't like the way his gaze worked its way the length of her body. She was conscious that beneath her robe she had on only her underwear. And the gun in her pocket.

She pointed toward the living room to their right. "Why don't you have a seat in the living room, Agent Selby, and I'll get the box." She left him and worked her way back down the foyer to the library. An uncomfortable doubt nagged her about handing over the manuscript to him. The Monroe police had okayed it, but she simply didn't like Selby.

He was sitting on the velvet Victorian couch in front of the fireplace when Brenda handed him the FedEx box. She sat down in the wing chair opposite him. Selby peeked inside the box, then set it beside him, his gaze intense.

"First, I'd like to get a better start with you than at our first meeting at your office." He paused and Brenda thought he expected her to say something. When she didn't, he continued, "I'm sure Detective Reccio told you we needed some answers from you regarding the manuscript and Heather Ritter. The quicker we're done, the sooner I can be on my way."

"I'd like that, thank you, but first, tell me why is the FBI so desperate to get the manuscript?" It was something she'd wondered from the beginning. She smiled, wanting desperately for Steven Selby to be out of Malfour.

He leaned forward and clasped his hands. "This manuscript is valuable evidence. It may the missing piece that might crack the case, Ms. Strange. There are many things and people involved. It's very complicated." He paused. "Now, tell me why you went back a second time to visit Hilda Moran the day of her murder."

"You mean why I disobeyed your FBI order to stay away from the case?" Brenda realized it was a sarcastic response and prolonged Selby's presence in her house, but it had just tumbled out.

Selby just smiled, but it wasn't a happy face. "Hilda Moran could have been murdered by the men you accidentally stumbled across."

"Or maybe I saved Heather and Matt Ritter's lives by being there?" Brenda had never given that any thought, but it made sense now that she brought it up. "Look, Agent Selby, I do want to help out in catching whoever murdered both Clifford Satterly and Hilda Moran, but I'm not your suspect. I'm a PI. I had unfinished business with Hilda. She had had important dealings with my client. I thought she could answer some more questions for me."

Selby smiled, showing even, white teeth. "Can you describe the fake Detective Garbano or any of the men on the scene?" He cocked his head, holding the smile.

That scene was something Brenda had wanted to purge from

her brain. Now this FBI agent was asking her to bring back the sight of blood and the smell of it. Would he believe her if she told him she saw the vision of Hilda sprawled in a pool of blood without actually being in the room?

"Garbano was short, with dark hair graying at the temples. His eyes and complexion were dark, olive-skinned. I assumed he was Hispanic or Italian. His clothes were rather casual. He had on nice pants and a denim shirt. It looked like he'd been pulled off a golf course."

"Any logos on the shirt or pants, an alligator or the Polo horse?"

Brenda didn't remember any logos on Garbano's clothes.

"How about an accent?" Selby continued. "Did he have an accent?"

Brenda shook her head. "None."

"And they didn't allow you into the crime scene?"

"No."

"Did you hear anything? Something that might be important?"

"I spoke very little to Garbano, or whoever the hell he is, before someone called him back inside. He said he'd be calling me to ask me some questions but he never did."

Selby sat back on the couch. "Thank you, Ms. Strange. I've been through the real Monroe County police report, but can you tell me how you came to have this manuscript dropped in your lap?"

"I spoke to Heather Ritter and her son the day of Hilda's murder. They weren't of much help then, but I left them my card. Heather called me and said she wanted to hire me. She admitted she had been at Hilda's house the day FedEx delivered the package. Aware of Hilda's work with valuable autographs, Heather bet that the package contained something valuable, something she could sell to put her son through college. She forged Hilda's signature. I told her I couldn't take her case and urged her to go to the police, turn over the manuscript and tell them the whole story. She showed up at my office instead. I don't believe she knew what was inside that box. Panicked by what had happened to Hilda, she wanted no part of the manuscript. That's why she left it with me. She's a very frightened woman."

"Where are Heather Ritter and her son now?" Selby didn't remove his gaze from Brenda.

"I assume they're back in Homestead. She left the note that's in the box."

Agent Selby dug out the handwritten note, scanned it quickly, then stuck it back in the FedEx box. He set his green eyes once more on Brenda. "Ms. Strange, I don't need to remind you again that this case is in the hands of the Monroe County police and the FBI, not to mention that it's a dangerous case. Once I leave with this package, I hope we won't have to meet again."

Brenda got up. She'd had enough. "My sentiments exactly." She'd given Selby all the information she had. They knew where to find her.

Selby got up, the box balanced in one hand, his other hand outstretched toward Brenda. "Thank you, Ms. Strange, for your cooperation."

Brenda, thankful to be rid of him, ushered him out into the foyer, but Selby stopped in midstride.

"By the way, Ms. Strange, did you take a look at the manuscript?" He held up the box, a slight smirk curling the side of his lips. "It's human nature to be curious."

Brenda immediately thought of the copy in the library. She gave him one of her most unassuming smiles. "That doesn't sound like a question relating to this investigation."

Selby shook his head. "No, it isn't."

Brenda handed him his still soaked raincoat and watched him get into the blue Chrysler and drive off. The rain had petered out into a drizzle, but the sky remained a solid dark gray, and angry rumbles of thunder shook the air. The palm trees drooped, soaked from the initial onslaught of rain. And the air had turned chilly.

Brenda wrapped the robe tighter around her waist and went back inside. She couldn't help but wonder what would happen to the Malenko manuscript now. Would it go back to the FBI with Steven Selby or pause at the Monroe County Sheriff's Office? It was officially out of her hands. But could she let it go so easily? She wondered about Heather and Matt Ritter. Questions remained about the real power of the Malenko manuscript and she was still curious as to who Conrad Malenko was.

She was about to go back to her copy of the manuscript when her cell phone chirped. It was Cubbie.

"I'm not going to take no for an answer, boss lady. Be ready in thirty minutes, 'cause I'm pickin' you up for dinner. You need a break away from work and that house."

Brenda couldn't stop the smile on her face. "You're assuming I haven't had dinner yet?" She hadn't. And she was hungry. A glance at her watch told her it was 5:45.

"Sugar, I know you better than I know some of my folks. You think you've built some kinda mystery around yourself, but you're transparent to me, honey. Be ready when I beep my horn."

Brenda flipped the phone shut, looked at the pages of the manuscript neatly piled on the library sofa and sighed. The manuscript would have to wait. She really was hungry.

The barely perceptible ringing of her cell phone woke Brenda from a deep sleep, the best sleep she'd had in nights. She reached groggily for the phone on her nightstand. God, she hoped it wasn't Cubbie. They'd just had dinner the night before. Brenda wasn't eager to hear any more admonishments from Cubbie about the Malenko manuscript.

"Ms. Strange?" It was a man's voice.

Brenda didn't recognize it right away.

"Ms. Strange, it's Detective Reccio with the Monroe County Sheriff's Office. Can you hear me?"

Brenda sat up, brushed some loose strands of hair from her face and swallowed. There was a sick feeling in her stomach.

"What's wrong, Detective?"

"Agent Selby is missing and so is that manuscript he was supposed to bring back."

Even though Brenda knew there were birds chirping outside and a light breeze blowing through the trees, her world went completely silent.

"Ms. Strange? Did you hear me? I need to ask you some questions regarding Agent Selby's visit with you."

Brenda jerked back into reality. She shook her head hard to get rid of the murky slush that was in her brain. "Agent Selby left here at about five-thirty yesterday evening. I assumed he was on his way back to you."

"Well, he never made it back here or anywhere else, apparently. We've put out an APB and a missing persons alert. The FBI has got people tracking his whereabouts."

Brenda couldn't suppress the shivers that rippled through her body. The Malenko manuscript was missing again. "What about the car?" she asked.

"It hasn't been found. That doesn't necessarily mean anything, just that both man and car have disappeared. But we've got the tag number."

There was really nothing she could do. She told Detective Reccio the questions Selby asked her and everything else she remembered. Detective Reccio thanked her and warned her he might be calling again. Then he rang off.

Brenda got out of bed and headed for the shower. A hot shower. Besides a massage by Tina or making her bears, that was the closest thing to relaxing her at times like this. Well, that or a strong martini.

Yesterday's rain had left the morning fresh and clear. From the large window in her bedroom, Brenda marveled at the breathtaking beauty outside. The waters of the bay inlet sparkled like gems under the bright sun and the palm trees swayed to the caress of a light breeze. It was going to be a beautiful Thursday.

But Brenda couldn't quiet the storm that was raging in the pit of her stomach. She dressed in black sweater, tan pants and black boots, went down to the kitchen and fixed herself a cup of hot raspberry tea. At last she slowed down enough to realize Butterscotch had no food in his dish. She poured out the Science Diet special dry food for kittens and filled his water dish to the top.

The phone call from Detective Reccio had changed her itinerary. Now more than ever, she knew she had to find the secret to the Malenko manuscript. She no longer doubted that powerful forces were at work behind the mysterious book. But more than searching for esoteric secrets, what she craved at that moment was the sound of Tina's voice. But talking to Tina would have to wait. Tina would be in the middle of work. She wouldn't have the time to talk. Brenda would call later tonight. This morning, her job was to find a Russian translator.

Chapter Twelve

Coincidentally, Professor Boris Romakoff was head of the language department at South Tampa University, Tina's next place of employment beginning in September. This was the perfect opportunity for Brenda to get a look and feel for the place. Just after ten, she reached the professor, who acted very interested in the manuscript. Unfortunately, he couldn't see her before 1 p.m., so they arranged to meet then.

Brenda called Cubbie, told her she wouldn't be in today and to forward any calls regarding the Malenko manuscript to her cell phone.

South Tampa University was a gorgeous campus, small but lavish in its Art Deco architecture and perfectly manicured grounds. It wasn't too difficult to find. Brenda had taken Kennedy Boulevard to Westshore, turned right to Cypress and then a left toward the water. STU stood at the end of a jutting finger of sand dotted with palm trees at the edge of Tampa Bay. The towering Howard Franklin Bridge was visible in the distance.

At the center of the campus was the student services building. Brenda inquired about the language department and was directed to a coral-colored building across the wide expanse of lawn. Although it was a perfect Florida March day, while crossing the carpet of soft grass she couldn't suppress a slight shiver. Why this sense of foreboding in the middle of a sunlit day? And was it her imagination, or did a long shadow trail behind her?

She stopped and glanced over her shoulder but saw nothing except students going about their business. Feeling foolish but nonetheless apprehensive, she clutched the manila envelope containing the copy of the Malenko manuscript closer to her chest. Inside the languages building, she found Professor Romakoff's name on the directory and followed the door numbers down a hallway where students and faculty milled about.

Brenda found the door with Professor Romakoff's name in gold on a black plaque. She looked at her watch. She was early. So typical of her. She knocked first, then opened the door.

The small, cramped room was filled with books and several chairs. And a desk. The man sitting behind it wasn't exactly what she expected.

Professor Romakoff got up and offered a big smile and a hand. "You must be Brenda Strange."

He was maybe in his fifties, with blond hair now graying brushed back atop a wide forehead. His small, fashionable glasses didn't hide glimmering blue eyes.

Brenda took his hand. "It's a pleasure to meet you, Professor Romakoff."

"Have a seat, please." He motioned to one of the two empty chairs across from the desk. The others were stacked with textbooks.

"Thank you for taking the time to see me, Professor." Brenda settled into the old chair, the wood creaking beneath her.

The professor adjusted his glasses and smiled. "How could I refuse a look at a rare manuscript written by hand in Russian?"

The light was dim in the room, with only one window allowing a washed-out sprinkling of sunshine in. Brenda noticed a large map of the world on one wall.

The professor reached across his desk. "Now, let's see what you've got."

Brenda handed him the envelope and watched as he opened it and thumbed through the pages, stopping at the ones with the illustrations of the Baphomet Goat.

She slid closer to the edge of her seat. "I was hoping you could enlighten me on the meaning of the illustrations in particular."

Romakoff arched an eyebrow and glanced up at her. "Well, you were correct in assuming this was an occult treatise." He went back to the manuscript and turned more pages. "I'm not well versed in occult literature, but these pages leave no doubt as to the purpose of the book. The ritual described here is extreme, to say the least. Most would consider it quite gruesome." He stopped and looked up at her again. "I am certain of the translation. Conrad Malenko was seeking to make a deal with the devil in exchange for eternal life."

"Eternal life?" Brenda asked. "Like Ponce de León and the Fountain of Youth?"

Professor Romakoff shook his head. "No, no. Conrad Malenko seemed convinced he had all the powers at his disposal to accomplish his pact with the devil. According to this, it's my understanding that the most important ingredient for the success of the ritual was the five heads."

"Heads?" Shock jolted Brenda back into the seat. "The ritual calls for decapitation?" The word stung her nose with the scent of blood; pictures of a headless Hilda Moran and Clifford Satterly flashed through her brain like windblown snapshots.

Professor Romakoff continued riffling through the pages of the manuscript. "Yes. These are illustrations of the inverted pentagram." He tapped the page in front of him with his index finger. "Malenko would have to be inside this pentagram at all times during the ritual. At the five corners of the star, five severed human heads would offer more protection from the"—he paused, peering intently at the page—"the goat devil that was to grant him his wish. Four of the heads represent the elements of earth, wind, fire and water, and directions east, west, north and south. The fifth head would be an offering to the demon." He stopped abruptly. "Is Conrad Malenko alive?"

The question caught Brenda off-guard. A cold chill had suddenly paralyzed her in her seat. Both Clifford Satterly and Hilda Moran had been decapitated. Could Malenko really be alive and in search of heads for his depraved ritual? If so, they needed two more heads. Had Jim Varley's head been severed? Detective Reccio hadn't divulged that information.

She shook her head, partly to get the bloody images from her mind. "No one seems to know. He disappeared after Hitler's Germany was defeated. Apparently, he draws the interest of scholars and those in search of esoteric occult figures."

"Such as yourself?" He was smiling at her.

"Mine is a passing interest."

"Well, I can give you better reading material than this on truly interesting Russian figures in history."

"I'm afraid I have all I can handle, Professor, but thank you for your offer. And for your time."

Romakoff's face showed slight regret. "Ms. Strange, may I keep these pages overnight? I will be happy to personally deliver them to you tomorrow. I wouldn't mind reading the rest of the manuscript. As a professor of Russian language and studies, I'm a bit embarrassed at my unfamiliarity with Conrad Malenko."

"I'm sorry, Professor, I can't let you keep it." Brenda blurted her answer without thinking she might have sounded rude. But she wasn't about to tell a total stranger her reason why she couldn't let even a copy of the rare manuscript out of her sight. Had she become obsessed? Or merely careful? The true manuscript, if it was authentic, was once again missing. With the horrifying deaths of everyone connected with the unfinished book, Brenda just didn't feel comfortable leaving the only surviving copy in the possession of Professor Romakoff.

Romakoff shrugged and offered an outstretched hand. "Ah, well, thank you for the opportunity, then."

He handed her back the pages. The room suddenly became unbearably stuffy. Suffocating. She needed to get out. She slipped the manuscript back into the manila envelope and shook his hand.

"Thank you again," she said, practically running out the door, inhaling deeply the metallic but cooling air in the hallway.

There was a nasty feeling sitting in the pit of her stomach. She had to get away from here. In a hurry. She had to get home to Malfour. Something was calling her back.

But why?

Brenda didn't even think of stopping at Strange Investigations. She rushed back to Malfour, breaking most of the speed limits along the way.

When she pulled up in front of Malfour and got out, she saw a small brown package on the porch, leaning against the door. It wasn't a box but rather one of those bubble-filled mailers. It was too small to be what she was thinking of. The original Malenko manuscript.

Brenda picked it up and gently squeezed. Maybe a book? Her name was written in sweeping, shaky handwriting, trying to look elegant. This hadn't been delivered by the Post Office or any other delivery service. All packages were left at the guardhouse if she wasn't home to receive them. There were no stamps or meter strip and no return address. The only package she was waiting for was something from her father. Obviously, this wasn't it. Maybe Cubbie or Eddie Vandermast, her friend and accountant, had left it for her? But neither one of them had mentioned anything about coming to Malfour with a package. Brenda scanned her surroundings. Nothing looked out of place.

She hurried inside, nearly tripping over Butterscotch, who'd met her in the foyer. She bent down and stroked his soft fur. He arched his back in delight, blinked a few times and tried to lead her into the dining room. His food dish must be empty, she thought.

"Okay, baby. I hear you, you little bottomless pit."

She filled his dish with Science Diet, petted him again and headed for the library. Still clutching the package, she checked for messages. None. It was time to see what was inside the padded envelope.

She peeled open the top and cautiously peeked inside. It was a book. She took a deep breath. It was a hardcover edition of *Malenko and the Black Arts*. She exhaled as she looked inside the package, hoping there was some kind of note. Nothing. Who had left it at her door?

If there had been a dust jacket, it was long gone, but other than that, the book looked almost brand new. It showed no shelf wear for a book over fifty years old. Was this Arthur Clemens's own copy? Had he had a change of heart and loaned her his copy after all? But he didn't know where she lived. She couldn't recall exchanging addresses with him and he'd said he would call if his contact agreed to loan her a copy of the book. Brenda never would have given her personal address to him anyway. Any kind of business was conducted at Strange Investigations. That's why she opened her private investigations office, to avoid strangers knocking at Malfour's doors.

The book was bound in red cloth, the way they used to do it. The title was imprinted in silver along the perfectly straight spine. While Brenda was excited, she was also apprehensive. Until she found out who had set foot on her porch and left the book there, she wouldn't feel comfortable.

She opened the book and saw the inscription written in the same wobbly handwriting:

For Brenda Strange,
We were destined to meet.
Compliments of BC Corporation

BC Corporation? What the hell was BC Corporation? The

headache powder company? Brenda was sure she'd never done business with any company by that name. The tiny knots in her stomach suddenly turned into a big knotted ball. Someone knew who she was. They knew where she lived. Was she being followed? Brenda's heart was thumping hard and the thunder in her ears drowned out everything around her.

What if whoever had killed Clifford Satterly, Hilda Moran and poor Jim Varley was after her? Maybe they knew she had a copy of the Malenko manuscript? She shivered. Pushing aside the tiny trickle of fear seeping through her, she focused on the book in her hand.

She'd just flipped to the center, where several pages of photos beckoned, when the loud ringing of the phone made her jump.

"Hello, Ms. Strange. Got UPS here with a delivery from Raymond Strange." It was Tony at the guardhouse.

The package from her father. Brenda's stomach twitched. She'd almost forgotten the mysterious "something" her mother had left for her. "It's from Father. I'm expecting it." Now was a good time to ask him if anyone had come looking for her that could have left the Malenko bio. "Tony, was anyone here earlier for a delivery?"

"No, ma'am. I've been on duty all morning and the only delivery for you is from the UPS man heading your way."

Brenda thanked him and hung up. Still clutching the Malenko book, she met the UPS man at the front door.

"Brenda Strange?" The young man held a small box in his hand and an electronic pad in the other.

She signed for it. She walked back to the library, laid the Malenko bio on the large desk, and sat down on the vanilla cream leather sofa, box balanced on her lap.Her palms were moist. Why was she so nervous? Curious yet apprehensive at the same time, she pulled back the tape and opened the small box to find what looked like a diary inside.

It was bound in tan leather, with three initials embossed in gold on the front cover. *NSW*. Nancy Winters Strange. Her mother's monogram. It was odd that her mother had left Brenda her private diary. She hadn't even known her mother kept one. She sighed and looked at the two books. Which one to read first?

The shrill ring of the phone jolted Brenda from her thoughts. She reached for it before it rang a second time.

"Princess?" It was Tina. Her voice brought the aching back into Brenda's heart. She missed her lover.

"This is a surprise, honey. Are you on break?" It was the middle of the afternoon. Tina usually called in the evening when she got home from the college and doing errands or shopping.

"Well, I just wanted to let you know that I'm trying to get out of here early for spring break. I want us to have more time together." She paused. Brenda could almost see the impish grin on her face. "Besides, I can't wait to see the gallery."

Brenda couldn't help but smile at the excitement in Tina's voice. "It looks great, baby. But it isn't complete without your art in it. When do you think you'll be coming home?" Her heart fluttered.

"Hard to say. The college lets out on the twenty-eighth of March, but I'm trying to convince the director to let me sneak out of here earlier, if I can."

"I can't wait to hold you, Tina." Brenda's voice was hoarse with desire.

"I'll never leave again, Princess. I'll be home soon, and after this semester, forever."

That sounded so good. Forever together. Brenda let it sink in and travel through her system like a drug. It made her high.

Tina agreed to call again when she had a definite date and flight plan. Reluctantly, they said good-bye.

Brenda decided to fix herself a light supper of sautéed vegetables and rice and, after the news, sought the comfort of her bed early. The day had left her drained. With Butterscotch firmly tucked under the comforter next to her, she chose to open her mother's diary first. Heissman's biography of Malenko might bring the horrifying nightmares back. She wasn't about to go looking for them.

Brenda ran her fingers over the raised letters on her mother's diary. Shoving aside the last memories of her mother's body wasting away from cancer, Brenda opened the diary. The first thing that struck her was that her mother had meticulously created a table of contents, listing subject matter with page numbers. Like a book.

Her gaze stopped at a chapter titled "Does Brenda have 'it'?" Perplexed as to what "it" might be, she turned to page one. She never realized how neat and lovely her mother's handwriting had been.

There was a date on the top left-hand corner of the page. Two days after Timmy's death.

It's with a heavy heart and sick stomach that I start this diary. I've never been able to express myself very well. I don't like to, actually. Contact with others is not something I openly seek or embrace. My husband is a necessity. A rung in the ladder of my climb to wealth and comfort. I need Raymond to satisfy what society expects of me. My children are the only special things in my life. I tried in vain to be more open with them. To show Timmy and Brenda how much love I have for them. But I was trying to tap a vein that would not bleed. And now Timmy is dead. My therapist tells me starting this diary will help me understand what happened and what is happening. But I don't think I really need a diary to tell me what happened and what's happening. I think that my daughter has the Winters gift. My family's psychic vision. I don't want to dwell on it for fear my heart would break beyond repair, but in looking back, I think that Brenda somehow knew or had "seen" the events that led to Timmy's death. She just didn't know what to do with the gift. I suppose that was my fault. I should have been more diligent in looking for signs of its manifestation. I should have talked to her about her inheritance. I'll become even sicker remembering all the signs that were there from the first time Raymond bought the tricycle for my little boy. Brenda started screaming the first time she set eyes on the tricycle. Raymond and I thought she was acting childish, selfish. Not wanting Timmy to have something she didn't have. She would wake us all at night screaming, tears running down her cheeks. She wouldn't tell us what her nightmares were about. She'd just sit there, balled up tight on her bed, and shake her head. I threatened to take her to a child psychologist, but Raymond didn't want to hear that.

And that's why when Brenda started screaming her head off outside that Sunday, I hesitated. I never bothered to look. God help me. I never looked . . .

She was there again. In her backyard, with her dolls all sitting pretty in their tiny chairs around the small table. It was Sunday. Every Sunday Brenda had teatime with her dolls and one stuffed teddy bear. And like he did each Sunday, Timmy rode his bike. The sound of his tricycle squeaked in her ears. He would circle slowly around her table of dolls while Brenda screamed. Her little brother hadn't touched any of his toys since getting the wretched thing. She remembered now. She had hated that tricycle. Way before the car crumpled it up like a piece of newspaper and Timmy with it. So she screamed. Why had she disliked the shiny red tricycle? The images continued to flicker in her head. Timmy headed toward the street. Toward the screeching car.

"Timmy!" The scream stuck in her throat and she bolted upright in bed, the room pitch dark, the echo of her brother's name fading. Butterscotch had jumped with fright at her abrupt waking from the nightmare. He blinked at her from the floor, his disapproval obvious from the pinned-back ears.

Brenda exhaled, letting go of the frightened breath she'd been holding, and sat quiet, waiting for her heart to stop thumping in her throat.

She'd fallen asleep. Her mother's diary lay open, facedown on the bed beside her. She couldn't suppress a shiver. The room was ice-cold. It was March in Florida. It shouldn't be this frigid in the house. She looked around for Carlotta or Angelique, but their familiar gray forms were nowhere to be found.

Brenda couldn't stop shaking. It was six forty-five a.m. and light out. What she needed was coffee. She picked up Butterscotch and hugged him tight.

"Didn't mean to give you a scare, baby boy." *I just meant to scare myself half to death.* Brenda wrapped her favorite chenille robe tight around her waist and headed downstairs for some strong Pumpkin Spice coffee. She'd bought several pounds of it at the Borders' bookstore last October and kept it in the fridge. It was always one of her seasonal favorites; she wished they offered it all year round. She hoped the coffee would clear up her brain. She needed to make sense of her mother's words and of her own new, slowly growing guilt. Had she really known Timmy's fate before it happened? Could she have prevented her little brother's death?

She filled up Butterscotch's food dish as the coffee brewed. She couldn't let herself become obsessesed by her mother's diary. Too many other things loomed larger and more threatening in her life. The Malenko manuscript was still missing and so was FBI agent Steven Selby. Someone had mysteriously left the Conrad Malenko biography at her doorstep and Tina was coming home. Coming back to Malfour where she belonged, she thought, smiling. Just then, the phone rang. It was nearly seven thirty.

It was Cubbie, or a very poor imitation. Her voice was weak and raspy. "Brenda, honey, I won't be able to get to the office this morning. Been sick as a dog all night."

"Don't worry about it, Cubbie, you just take care of yourself. Do you need anything I can pick up for you? I can be at your place as soon as I shower."

What sounded like an attempt at laughter ended in a coughing fit at the end of the line. "No, no, sweetie, I'll be fine. Just a bad sinus infection, I think. I get these once in a blue moon. I hate to miss work on Friday. If you need me tomorrow, I can come in on Saturday. This sinus stuff only keeps me down for a day or so." Cubbie wheezed into the phone. "Hope I didn't call too early, but

I got to feeling drowsy and thought I should call before I went back to sleep. You gonna be okay without me?"

"I'll be fine. Take a nice long weekend and I'll see you Monday morning. You get back into bed."

Brenda set down the cup of coffee and sighed, certain she was feeling the strains of fatigue. Calling Detective Reccio was at the top of her list. Had they found Steven Selby and the Malenko manuscript? She also wanted to read more of the Conrad Malenko bio, *Malenko and the Black Arts*. She had to call her father too. She still worried about him all alone at Monte Point. It was a large estate. She just didn't like the idea of her father living there all alone. She resolved to keep closer contact with him.

Brenda showered, dressed and decided to head out to Strange Investigations. Later, she'd check again with Felice at Teddies by the Park. Brenda had promised her the next Zodiac miniature bear, Pisces. That was another thing nagging her. She was behind in her bear making. She had enough fabric cut for five bears but no time or the drive to finish even one. She made a mental note to work on the bears this weekend. She could squeeze that in between her reading of her mother's diary and the Malenko bio. Surely that was something she could accomplish. She wasn't actively working on a case. She had more than enough time to put her mind to making five bears.

Try as she might, she couldn't take her thoughts from what she'd read in her mother's diary. What was the psychic power she spoke about? And what did it have to do with her mother's family, the Winterses?

As Brenda worked her way onto Bayshore Boulevard and turned on Swan Avenue where Teddies in the Park and Strange Investigations were located, she knew she would be spending more time with her mother's diary than with the Malenko bio.

As soon as she turned onto the side entrance that brought her to the back parking lot of her office, she got slammed with a strong feeling that something was wrong. She pulled into her parking place and flew out of the car. The door to Strange Investigations was ajar.

The sick feeling in the pit of Brenda's stomach didn't feel good. She approached slowly, inching the door open, making sure not to touch anything. Immediately she knew she'd been broken into. Chairs were overturned and books lay scattered on the floor, flung from their bookshelves. Cubbie's desk was a mess. There were papers strewn around the desk.

Brenda stared her violated office, suspecting who had done this and why. They were looking for the Malenko manuscript. She worked her way around Cubbie's desk, noticing that the drawers were pulled open and the contents spilled onto the floor. But the color television was still there. This had not been a robbery. She felt sure she would find the small security safe in the file room broken into. It wasn't broken into, it was gone. They had taken the safe and all the contents. It had only been a tabletop safe. Brenda didn't think she'd need anything bigger. She had stored all the Clifford Satterly paperwork in the safe as well as other pertinent papers relating to earlier cases.

She dreaded going into her private office. She always locked her door, but sure enough someone had skillfully pried the lock open with no damage at all to the beautiful pebbled glass. Inside, her office had been ravaged as well. Papers lay in heaps everywhere, her expensive law books slammed on the floor. Thankfully, she kept nothing personal in her office. Strange Investigations was merely a place for her to keep clients and people away from Malfour House.

Nonetheless, she felt as though she'd been personally violated. Again. When she and Tina moved into Malfour, they'd had break-ins. The thought of strangers leaving their energy in her home was a repulsive feeling she'd never been able to let go of. And now it was happening again here.

Brenda knew she should call the police, but she wasn't so sure she wanted them involved. This wasn't a random act. The

Malenko manuscript wasn't here so whoever broke in wouldn't be back. She couldn't explain why she knew that, she just did.

Brenda opted not to call Cubbie. Definitely not Cubbie. If she knew someone had broken into Strange Investigations because of the Malenko manuscript, she just might pack up her bags and go back to waiting tables at the Gulfbreeze.

It would take all day, but Brenda decided to clean up the mess herself and buy a better deadbolt for the door. But then the realization hit her. If they were desperate enough to break into Strange Investigations, would Malfour House be next? And if the people in search of the Malenko manuscript still hadn't found it, what had happened to Steven Selby?

Chapter Thirteen

It had taken her the better part of the day to put everything in order, and by the time she finished discussing her Zodiac Bears with Felice, it was nearly three in the afternoon. Brenda had yet to call Detective Reccio, let alone stop for lunch. She was hungry, but she was hungrier for news, any kind of news, on the missing Steven Selby and the manuscript.

There was a certain sense of urgency inside her, all of it converging on Malfour House. She decided to skip lunch, head back home and call Detective Reccio from there. Then she would check in on Cubbie and see how she was feeling.

Tony Cutcheon was on duty when Brenda pulled up. Now was a good time to ask him more questions about the new neighbor. Tony was the only one who'd seen the limo after the movers left. Always on the lookout for a chance to help her out on cases, he usually passed her on without asking for the resident pass.

Now Brenda rolled down the window of her gold Jaguar as

Tony walked to the side of the car. She smiled at his enthusiasm. And to think she hadn't liked him at first meeting.

"Hi, Tony. I got to thinking of my new neighbor at the Davis house and thought you might be able to help me out."

"Anything I can do, Ms. Strange."

"You mentioned a black limo and big moving trucks—you don't by any chance remember any name on the moving trucks or license plates?"

He rubbed his nonexistent chin. "I know the trucks weren't the popular movers that you see around." He paused and thought some more, finally breaking into a big grin. "Carriage Movers. And the plates were from New York." Tony eyed Brenda intently. "Are you going to check them out?"

Brenda smiled back. "It's a big help, Tony. Thanks."

"You bet. Hold on right there." He took off back into the guardhouse and came back with a piece of paper with a name he'd scribbled. Brad Smith. "This is how he spells his name. In case you need it."

Brenda stashed the paper in her handbag. "Have you met Brad Smith yet?"

"Not really. He came in a limo and the driver handed me the information we keep on file here. I never got a good look at Mr. Smith."

Doubt niggled at Brenda. She didn't know why. "What did the driver of the limo look like? Does Brad Smith travel much?"

"The limo driver is a big, bulky guy. The Sylvester Stallone type, you know. And at least on my shifts, I've only seen them that once, and that's it."

She smiled again at Tony. "Thanks again. You're a big help." Tony waved her on, his face beaming. He was turning out be an invaluable aid to her.

With her interest piqued about the new owners of the former Stewart and Joan Davis house, once over the inlet bridge Brenda continued on Tide Boulevard instead of turning on Sea Breeze Lane and home to Malfour. She thought she'd take one peek around the old neighborhood and check out who her mysterious, rich new neighbor, Brad Smith, might be.

She hadn't been at the Davis house since December. As she slowed down and rolled toward the front of the palatial home, her jaw dropped. The sun was fading in the March Florida sky, and the house appeared to stand naked in the growing darkness. The change was startling. The landscaping had been stripped of all the extravagances Stewart and Joan had built into it. The grounds were overgrown, unkempt. The bubbling fountain at the front entrance was empty of water, weeds sticking out from where once colorful lights shimmered on the water. The giant marble columns that had once made the house look like an ancient Roman palace now made the mansion look like a ruined temple. There was an air of neglect about the place.

There were no cars parked in the long winding entrance and the window shades were all drawn. Reclusive, she thought. There was negative energy coming from the place. It was hitting her square in the gut.

She sped up and passed the house, not wanting to look suspicious in case someone was peeking out from somewhere inside. She would be glad to get back to the welcoming arms of Malfour.

But as soon as she walked through her front door, a blast of icy air slammed her face and the whisper in her ear was urgent. "Leave, Brenda. You are in danger!" It was Carlotta.

Brenda searched the foyer for her ghostly companion, but she was nowhere to be seen. "Carlotta, what's going on? Where are you?"

"He's searching the house. The evil old man. We're hiding from his eye. You must hide too."

Carlotta was beginning to scare her. Angelique was always the drama queen and the playful one. Carlotta was dead serious.

"Hiding from his eye? I'm not going anywhere until the both of you tell me what you're talking about." Brenda plopped her large handbag on the foyer table, alert to the silence of Malfour. If there was someone here, he was invisible.

"He's gone, Brenda. Carlotta is still in a flurry about it."
Angelique, in her saucy 1920s flapper haircut and deathly gray
complexion, took form beside Brenda.

"He has left his darkness behind and I was trying to warn
Brenda." Carlotta, blond curls falling to her shoulders against an
equally gray complexion, appeared next to Angelique, a frown on
her pale lips.

Brenda shook her head and put one hand up. "Will you two
settle down and one of you tell me what is going on? Was someone
in Malfour? Did they break in?" Suddenly realizing the potential
danger, Brenda thought maybe she should check the house out.

"Yes," Carlotta answered.

"No," Angelique said with conviction. "Carlotta is exaggerat-
ing. No one broke in. But there was someone here."

"Spying. Intruding into all of your private things," Carlotta said
in a rush, evidently not wanting to get interrupted by Angelique.

Brenda didn't want to take any chances, so she left Angelique
and Carlotta and began a thorough search of Malfour House. Both
her ghostly friends accompanied her, popping up and offering bits
of meaningless information. Brenda found no signs of breaking
and entering and, after looking through all her drawers, cabinets
and boxes, found nothing out of order. If someone had been here
rifling through her things, they'd taken an awful lot of time
making sure everything was as she'd left them. And nothing was
missing. The copy of the Malenko manuscript, which she'd immediately suspected her intruder was after, still sat in her cedar chest
where she'd put it for safekeeping. What were Carlotta and
Angelique talking about?

Brenda took a hot shower, fixed a large spinach salad for dinner
and a Belvedere vodka martini to go with it. All she could get out
of Carlotta and Angelique over dinner was that they "sensed"
another presence in the house. She'd had the best intentions of
working on the Pisces zodiac bear and calling Detective Reccio,
but she couldn't stop thinking of her mother's diary that waited for
her upstairs and the Malenko biography right next to it.

❧

Nancy Winters Strange Diary, February 24, 1978

I finally have to admit to myself that Brenda has the Winters psychic gift. I can't deny it any longer. She got what should have been mine. I always felt cursed because the power bypassed me and now I know why. At Brenda's 10th birthday party, for reasons I didn't know at the time, she insisted her party be held indoors. I had already made extensive and expensive preparations for a gala affair with clowns, ponies and a miniature train ride in our backyard, weather allowing. She must have known what was going to happen that day. Just like she did with Timmy. She just didn't understand. Couldn't comprehend all the signals going through her young mind or channel the psychic potential at her fingertips. I should have explained the Winters gift of psychic powers to her, but I admit I was selfish and bitter. I didn't want her to have it. I wasn't going to help her. The day of her birthday party turned out to be one of the worst February storms in Tarrytown. The snow fell then turned to slush and icy rain. It had come out of nowhere. We do get bad storms at this time of the year, but nothing like this was forecast. I had provided a large circus tent for the affair, in case of some light snow. The weather forecasters were stumped, but Brenda had known. Too bad I hadn't listened to her. How could I? I was cheated. The Winters gift has only skipped three generations and I was one of them. Well, she can have it. I know in her head she continues to blame me for Timmy's death, but I have come to grips with the realization that it wasn't me after all. I suffered a great deal after my little boy died. Raymond doesn't know the half of it. I nearly went insane. I wanted to die. I wanted to dig the earth over Timmy's grave and crawl into that dark coffin with him and never come back. There were moments, many moments, I'm ashamed to say, when I looked at Brenda and wished her dead instead of Timmy. God help me, but I did. She had the power and I think I hated her for it and I hated her for Timmy.

Drip. Drip, drip. Brenda woke up and wiped the wet drops off her arm. Damn, she thought, was the roof leaking? As she fumbled

107

for the night-light, she noticed Butterscotch cowering beneath the chair near the window.

She flipped the switch on the lamp and saw blood splattered on her arm, staining the sheet. Blood was everywhere—sliding down her walls, clotting in a thick maroon pool on the floor and dripping from the ceiling. Malfour was drowning in blood.

She screamed and rubbed her eyes and opened them again. The blood was gone. The room was back to normal. Butterscotch, firmly settled on the bed beside her, blinked in curiosity. Her mother's diary lay open beside her. Brenda swallowed hard to get her heart back down into her chest.

She must have fallen asleep reading the diary. Had her mother's words brought on that horrifying dream? What did it mean? Was she in danger? An overwhelming feeling of sadness suddenly overcame her. Her mother had lived a bitter and angry life. And that anger had been directed at Brenda. What irony, she thought. Since Timmy's death, Brenda had tried to cope with her own feelings of blame toward her mother, and now to find out her mother had distrusted her.

Worse was the guilt and despair that had gathered inside her after reading the diary. They sat in her heart like chunks of concrete. Had she been able to save Timmy? Surprisingly, Brenda found she didn't want to dwell on that. She simply couldn't allow herself to even consider it. If she did have the Winters psychic gift, she hadn't known it at the time. There was nothing she could have done. Nothing.

She knew she had to make herself get busy if she wanted to avoid the demons gathering at her mind's door—demons that right now were edging her toward a vodka martini. She dismissed the thought from her head and decided instead for an early-morning coffee. Dawn was peeking through the curtained windows of Malfour. Her clock radio read six a.m. Maybe she could check on how Cubbie was doing? It was Saturday. Most people sleep in on the weekend, so she'd wait till later in the day to call her.

Brenda decided to just shower, dress, grab a bagel and head out to her office. She had to phone Detective Reccio and wanted to make sure the place was safe after the break-in. As she drove in the cool March morning, the hurt of missing Tina hit hard. It was already March twentieth and she hadn't heard whether she would be able to come home early for spring break. If Brenda could cross her toes, she would. She was desperate for her lover.

When she pulled into the parking lot, she spotted Cubbie's old VW Bug. What was she doing at work? Thankful that Cubbie was feeling good enough to be at work, but fearful of another break-in or something else gone wrong, Brenda trotted to the front door.

"Wow, boss lady, what in blazes are you doing here on a Saturday?" Cubbie looked like something left over from a bad party. Her eyes were puffed up, her nose redder than Rudolph's.

Brenda noticed the slightly wrinkled tailored blouse and the missing baseball hat. "I love you too, Cubbie. I was worried about you. Glad to see you're better, but I should ask you the same thing. You didn't have to come in today, you know. I meant to call last night."

"Yeah, yeah, I know. You got busy. I know you, sweetie. I take good care of myself, don't you worry. I just get antsy at home with nothin' to do. You forget that I waited tables all my life. I can't tell you the long hours I put in at the Seabreeze." Cubbie winked. "I'd rather be here, sugar."

Brenda quickly scanned the office for anything out of place or suspicious. She was suddenly conscious of the bag with the bagel in her hand. She'd only gotten one for herself. She hadn't planned on Cubbie being here. "I'm sorry, but I only picked up one bagel. I didn't think—"

"That's okay, honey, I fixed myself something at home before coming in." Cubbie took the bag from Brenda and headed for the file room, which also served as their coffee break room. "I'll butter this up and fix us both some coffee."

"Extra strong this morning, please," Brenda said as she worked her way to her office. "I've got some calls to make."

Brenda sat down at her desk and tried to erase the images of her office the way it had looked yesterday morning. She didn't ever want to go through that again. And she didn't want to put Cubbie in a potentially dangerous position. Brenda was sure that whoever had broken in was a professional and was somehow connected to the Malenko manuscript. There wasn't even an attempt to break into Felice's teddy bear shop at the front of the house. Felice kept her cash box right under the front counter.

Detective Reccio was first on her list of calls to make. Something was amiss in FBI agent Steven Selby's disappearance. Next, she wanted to try and locate Carriage Movers in New York. She might not know who Brad Smith was, but at least she might find out where he came from. If they wouldn't give her information over the phone, then maybe Kevin at the New Jersey detective agency might be able to do some legwork for her.

Cubbie came in holding a china plate, the bagel nicely toasted and buttered, napkins and a mug of steaming coffee. "Here you go, boss lady. I'll be at my desk if you need me." She was almost out the door but stopped. "By the way, what happened to the safe? Did you take it home or something?"

Damn. Brenda had completely forgotten about the safe. She had to think fast. "I didn't think that safe was secure enough. I decided to replace it with something better. I'll probably pick one up this weekend."

Cubbie shrugged. "Whatever you say, boss." Thank God she didn't question it. She started to walk away.

"Hey," Brenda said, "do I need to get you a new cap or are you just having another bad hat day?" She couldn't get used to Cubbie's bare head and unruly, shoulder-length red curls.

Cubbie sniffled and wiped her nose with a Kleenex. "I still got a bit of a sinus headache and those hats just make it worse. I got plenty of caps, sugar." She laughed and walked away.

Brenda couldn't suppress a smile as she punched in Detective Reccio's number on her phone.

"Reccio."

Brenda recognized his gravelly voice. "Good morning, detective. It's Brenda Strange in Tampa."

"Sorry, Ms. Strange, but I've got nothing new on the agent's disappearance. They're doing their best to keep us in the dark, but my contacts tell me the agency is stumped. One thing you might find interesting, though, is that apparently Agent Selby was known for working outside the box within the FBI, if you know what I mean."

"I don't know what you mean, detective."

"Evidently, Selby was able to slip and slide through several branches of the agency, including the U.S. Marshals foreign relations department. He spent lots of unaccounted time overseas."

Was she missing something? She wasn't connecting the dots. She couldn't even see the dots. "I don't see what this has to do with Steven Selby's disappearance along with the Malenko manuscript. I'm pretty convinced it all has to do with that manuscript."

Reccio paused. "I'm just passing along information you might find helpful, Ms. Strange. It may be nothing, but you should know that in police work, sometimes what may not seem like anything could lead to something. We don't overlook information."

They agreed to keep in touch if anything new turned up. The conversation left her feeling disheartened. Where was Selby and the manuscript? Did he steal it? Or was his decapitated body lying somewhere dark and lonely, the Malenko manuscript in the hands of the murderers who would stop at nothing to get it? How long would it take them to murder two more people for the satanic ritual outlined in Malenko's pages?

Without warning, the room began to dim into a dull, gray cloud, and the swirling sound in her ears was like the tide rushing to the shore. She got up slowly, fearing she might faint. Holding on to the edge of her desk, she could feel her heart racing. For one instant, she envisioned Malfour engulfed by complete darkness, falling into a black, hungry chasm, ready to swallow it whole.

"Cubbie." Brenda tried to remain calm.

Cubbie walked into the room and gasped. "Damn, sugar, what is going on?" She rushed over and steadied her with surprisingly strong hands. "Are you sick? You want me to take you to the hospital? Why don't you sit back down, honey?" She maneuvered her back into the chair behind the desk.

"Cubbie, that's okay. I'm all right. Just a dizzy spell, that's all." Brenda waved her off. She had to leave now. She couldn't ignore the alarms going off in her head. Something was wrong at Malfour and she had to go home.

She got up and this time, the room didn't move with her. Cubbie hovered by her side, her gaze intent on every move Brenda made.

"I don't think you should go anywhere just yet, boss lady."

"I'm fine. I've got to get back home."

"You just left. What could be so important that you'd risk another spell and pass out at the wheel or something?"

"There's something I forgot at the house. I'll be right back." Truth was, Brenda didn't know if she'd be back or not.

Cubbie shook her head. "No, I don't think I'm gonna let you do that. Let me drive you at least. Or call you a cab if you're so desperate."

Brenda squeezed past the immovable object that was Cubbie. "Cubbie, please, don't worry. I'm not dizzy anymore." She suspected she had to furnish Cubbie with plausible reasons for her condition. "I haven't been eating like I should and not sleeping well either. It just caught up with me, that's all."

Cubbie followed her out of the office. "I suppose I can't stop you, but promise me you'll call me when you get home. And stay there. Get some rest. Don't worry about a thing. Maybe we can get together on Sunday."

Brenda left, the feeling of danger growing with each red light that stood in her way. She broke every speed limit on the way and made it to the Tides in record time. It would have been helpful if Tony was at the guardhouse, but he wasn't, so she had to stop and show her resident ID to an unfamiliar guard.

As she approached Malfour, the house seemed too quiet against the blue sky, as if it were waiting for her. It made her skin crawl. Bringing the Jag to a screeching halt, she bolted into the Malfour foyer and consuming darkness. The walls that had been covered in ominous shadows were now completely consumed by the blackness. It was like going into a cave. Where were Carlotta and Angelique?

It was then Carlotta screamed into Brenda's head. "Leave now! There are evil men here!"

Brenda wanted to ignore her. Yesterday when Carlotta had reacted this way, Brenda could find nothing to support Carlotta's hysteria. But something was different this time.

Standing still in her own foyer, she was nearly knocked off her feet by two abrupt, strong bursts of cold air rushing through her body. A chill that went deep into her bones and her soul. Her teeth chattered wildly.

"Get out now, or we'll do it again, Brenda." Angelique's voice had lost its usual light and playful quality.

"What the hell is happening here?" Brenda spoke into the darkness.

Footsteps answered her. Ghosts didn't make those kinds of sounds. She couldn't tell where they were coming from or how many there were. Before she had time to react, a darker shadow moved within the shadows. Someone or something was in Malfour! Brenda cursed herself for not having her gun.

From the living room, several tall figures emerged and faced her in the hallway.

"Hello, Ms. Strange. This isn't the best way to meet again." Arthur Clemens flipped one of the light switches. He stood a few feet away, the light illuminating his Mephisto-like features. She hadn't seen him since last December at the autograph show in Ft. Lauderdale that Eddy, Tina and she had attended. Two other tall men waited behind him like bodyguards.

The fear inside Brenda crumbled in the inferno of rage burning through her.

"Get the hell out of my house." She lunged for his throat. She gripped the lapels of his black wool suit. Before she knew it, the two big brutes grabbed her, pinning her tightly between them. One of them wrapped a thick arm around her neck, wrenching her elbow up behind her.

She tried to pull away, squirming, kicking and struggling, all to no avail. The other big guy clamped her wrists with handcuffs. They were icy cold and bit into her flesh. Realizing she was beaten for the moment, anger and frustration coursing through her system like adrenaline, she decided to relax. She cast a steely glance at Clemens.

He had clearly enjoyed her struggle. She could tell by the gleam in his eyes and the slight curl on his mouth.

"We're not here to hurt you or your house. We're just going to take a little ride, that's all. Don't resist and you'll be fine. You will be blindfolded for the duration, of course."

He was so close to her that she could smell the stench of his cologne. She tugged uselessly against the handcuffs.

Clemens shook a finger at her. "No no. Don't make me punish you. It will be bad for you, Brenda Strange."

"Carlotta. Angelique!" Brenda called out. Where were they? She felt foolish asking for the help of ghosts. What could they do, anyway? Were they in hiding?

"Your ghosts don't frighten us. We knew they were here." Clemens sounded smug.

Brenda wanted so badly to just kick him in the balls—after punching his teeth in. But she couldn't move. Arthur Clemens dug out a roll of silver duct tape from his coat pocket, peeled off a long strip, tore it off in one quick motion and stuck it over her mouth. She tried to turn away, but one of the brutes jerked her head forward. From behind her, a black scarf was wrapped around her eyes then tied with a tight knot at the back of her head. She could hardly even blink behind the rough fabric.

Brenda decided to go along with them. She really had no choice. She knew that she wouldn't be able to make a break for it right now. Someone opened her front door and she was shuffled forward. The cool outside breeze felt good. Just as the four of them were out the door, the phone started ringing.

"Guess what," Arthur Clemens said snidely. "You're not home." He laughed out loud as she was brutally shoved forward.

Brenda caught the sound of a car pulling up and a car door opening. She tried resisting again, but the two brutes holding her had grips like steel.

She was shoved inside a car. The seat felt soft and plush. There was the slight scent of leather. An expensive car, Brenda thought. And it still had that new-car smell.

Someone sat down beside her. By the stink of the cologne, it was Clemens. Two more doors slammed shut and the car began to move.

Chapter Fourteen

They went up an elevator. She didn't need to see to know that. It was a smooth elevator, but there was no mistaking the sliding doors and lurch as it moved. Brenda was almost sure they were moving up. She was shuffled forward, shoved through a door, then slammed into an uncomfortable chair. Her blindfold was removed, tape ripped off her mouth and feet tied together. Her hands were cuffed behind the chair. She'd tried to gauge the distance from Malfour to wherever the hell she was, suspecting they might have deliberately gone in circles just to throw her off. Brenda was almost convinced they hadn't left the Tides. She would have known if they'd crossed the bridge by the way the car took the big gaps in the concrete. But if they were still in the Tides, where? The thought suddenly hit her like a hard punch. The new neighbor! This could be Stewart's old mansion! She glanced around the room. It sure as hell didn't look like the Davis mansion. Had Stewart and Joan even had an elevator? While she hadn't ever been given a tour of the house, she guessed the mansion was at least two or maybe three stories. Maybe they'd had a penthouse? If it was Stewart's place, perhaps this was where he'd hidden his illegal works of art?

The walls were painted red. Blood red. So startling was the effect that she barely heard Arthur Clemens walk out. The room was almost triangular in shape, similar to a pyramid, with a high, vaulted ceiling that rose to a point. And there were no windows. Had they been plastered over? She noticed two small vents at the top of the ceiling. The floor was shiny black, probably marble, she thought. There was no lighting, only two recessed bulbs high above, near the tip of the peaked ceiling. They faced each other, providing very little light below. This cast stark shadows in the room and on the walls, creating splotches of red. The color of old blood. The whole room brought back the vivid dream she'd had of blood pouring into Malfour. Had the dream been a warning?

"Everything comes down to the blood, doesn't it, Brenda?" The sinister, gravelly voice came from the recesses of the shadowy corners.

She strained to see into the darkness, not sure where it had come from. "Only cowards tie their hostage to a chair and then hide in the dark." Brenda hoped she sounded courageous and confident. This man knew her name yet she knew nothing. She was furious more than anything else, but she was also battling the tiny trickle of fear that was threatening to overtake rational thought. She had no desire to be the next head served up on a silver platter for some satanic ritual.

Emerging from the red shadows directly in front of her, a figure clad in an oversized black coat and slouch hat shuffled slowly forward and froze in the dim light beaming from overhead. Brenda couldn't see a face, just a pale chin with thin lips.

A picture clicked in her memory. A mental snapshot she had wanted to throw out. Standing in front of her was the same man who had stood in her backyard the day of that terrible thunderstorm! She no longer wondered where she was. She knew this was the man who had moved into the Davis house. She struggled against the tight ropes at her feet. Had he been the one who dared invade her home and brought her here against her will?

"Who the hell are you, you bastard?" she snapped. "I don't take well to situations where I'm at a disadvantage. You seem to know me, yet you've have taken great pains to remain hidden. I know you've trespassed on my property, and now you've added kidnapping to the report I'm going to file with the police." Brenda didn't think the threat of the police would frighten him, but it sounded good and made her feel somewhat empowered.

What might have been a chuckle escaped from the mysterious man in black, his teeth blackened, broken. How old was he? Was this who Carlotta and Angelique had warned her about?

"Why have you brought me here? If I'm a guest, then release me from this chair. If I'm a hostage, tell me why." Her fear had left, allowing a delicious anger to fill her up. "I'm not frightened of you or what you might do to me."

The same sound echoed from the man in front of her. "No, of course you don't feel the fear. You know what lies beyond. You've seen it. Felt the power that courses through the universe." Using a cane, he inched closer toward her, his steps short and slow. Was he handicapped?

He stopped about a dozen feet away, close enough for her to notice the scars and deep-set wrinkles creasing the lower part of his face. His chin was too narrow, coming to an almost sharp point.

"Very well, then, no more games. We are too old for that." From his pocket, a bony hand emerged bulging with thick blue veins. He pulled off the large black hat.

Brenda stared in shock at the sight of the man before her. It was hard to guess his age, but in the dim lighting, his shriveled skin made him appear like a walking mummy. His bald head was large, with small ears hugging sunken cheekbones, and from what she could tell, he had no eyebrows or eyelashes. In fact, he was devoid of any facial hair, not even a few gray stubbles.

But it was the eyes that snatched her attention. They burned with an obsidian intensity that most people would recoil from.

"I know you very well, Brenda Strange," he said. "I also know you have been many others." He paused. "Now allow me to introduce myself." He managed a feeble, stiff bow, which somehow seemed ridiculously macabre in this environment. "I am Conrad Malenko." He smiled, showing off his rotten teeth again. "I thought you would have figured that out long ago, given your choice of profession."

Why wasn't she surprised? After all, no one had ever confirmed his death. The realization of what he was after sent an icy chill through her. This wasn't a game.

"You've murdered three people for your manuscript—"

"Not for my manuscript. For eternal life," Malenko interrupted. "Those three people were not wasted, I assure you. They are going to play an important part in the greatest piece of black magic in the history of the arts. Brandon Satterly, Clifford's father, and his father before him were both Baphomet Chosen members. It was unfortunate for Clifford that he never found out and insisted on passing the manuscript around for others to see."

"So Clifford was telling the truth that he inherited the manuscript?" Brenda had never put faith in his explanation for having the manuscript.

"Two generations of Satterly men had been generous with their contributions to Baphomet Chosen. I allowed them to keep the manuscript in the strictest confidence until I needed it. It is unfortunate Brandon died before he could pass this information to Clifford. By the time we went in search of the manuscript, Clifford was trying to peddle it to anyone with enough cash."

"Why now?" Brenda asked. "You knew where the manuscript was all along."

Malenko swayed and leaned heavily on his cane for support. He inhaled deeply. "The black arts are like delicate mathematical equations. You can't just draw a pentagram on the floor, invoke the spirits and expect magic to happen. You must work with the laws of nature and the flow of the universe for your work to succeed. The ritual for eternal life can be performed only at a precise moment in history, the time when certain planetary configurations are perfectly aligned."

"Let me guess," Brenda said, "that time is right now."

Malenko nodded, his dirty smile widening. "You are correct, Brenda Strange. I have very little time before the period when I can perform my magic is forever gone. So you understand my urgency, then."

"What have you done with Agent Selby?"

Malenko wrinkled his face into a sneer. In the red darkness of the room, the vision of this ancient and evil man was unsettling.

"I've done nothing to or with Agent Selby. As a matter of fact, Steven has been an invaluable asset in my quest for immortality."

His words hung in the air. Brenda shook her head slowly. She should have known Selby was working for the devil. She'd suspected him from their first meeting.

"Selby brought you the manuscript, didn't he? It's what he was after all along. Does he even work for the FBI?"

"Oh, he works for the FBI. He wouldn't be of any use to me if he didn't. Baphomet Chosen, better known as BC Corporation, is a powerful worldwide group of magicians. The clout of the FBI working for us is invaluable."

"BC Corporation?" she asked. "You're BC Corporation?" She remembered the inscription on the book.

Malenko shook his head. "Tsk, tsk, Brenda. I truly overestimated you"—he paused and exhaled—"Baphomet Chosen. BC Corporation. We are the number two corporation in the world. Exporters and importers. Of everything human beings consume." He was pleased with himself, his grin wider. "If you'd read that book you were so hot for, you would have known. You also would have known why I had to destroy every copy known to exist, as well as anyone or anything that could reference that book. I own only a few boxes I choose to keep for amusement."

Brenda remembered something about Malenko heading some

organization in Germany patterned after the Knights Templar and their worship of the Baphomet devil goat. She hadn't had time to read the bio. Her mother's diary was more important.

This thing standing before her was more monstrous than she had imagined. "My bet is that you burned the publishing house and murdered the author. Did you also murder others connected with the book?" She shuddered at the answer she already knew.

"They were meaningless in the scheme of the universe, Brenda. You still don't understand."

She wanted the feeble Malenko to move in closer. She might be able to bring her tied-up feet right into his balls . . . or his chin. She didn't care if it toppled her onto the floor, anything was better than sitting there helpless, listening to the ravings of a lunatic.

Malenko hadn't moved. He stood perfectly still. Something glittered on his face, like sparkles of energy. Suddenly, his entire face burst with light and energy that shined from within and gathered in his now silver eyes. Eyes that fixed on her.

"Let me show you what I am." His voice echoed more powerfully. The scars and deep creases were bathed away in the bright gleam his whole head had become. His skull began to reflect beams of light, some brilliant, others more muted. There was no shadow left on his face; the features merged into a mask of hot light. It was as if he were engulfed in radiance.

His head suddenly flared, or so it seemed, into a visible aura that expanded out into the room, eating away at the darkness. For the merest instant, revealed inside that glowing aura, she could see the fabric of the universe. Vast expanses of black space, floating planets, human cells, wars, life and death all vibrated within it.

The room became whiter still and Brenda shut her eyes tight against the power she felt swirling around her. And in another instant, it was gone. Inky maroon darkness dripped into red. Brenda opened her eyes to see Conrad Malenko shaking visibly, eyeing her with an intense self-satisfaction.

"You see, Brenda, I am merely a magician balancing the secrets of the universe."

"All I see is a pathetic murderer."

Malenko's grin became a scowl. "I thought you were more intelligent. Or are you still blind? You traveled through that fabric of time and space, thrilled to the life energies within it. You know. You should be more advanced."

She had to concentrate on getting out of there. She needed him to come closer. Maybe if she angered him enough, he might let his guard down. She wondered where Clemens was.

Her chin in the air, she said, "I'm not impressed by your little parlor trick. David Copperfield could do better. Tell me what you want with me. You can still save yourself more trouble with the police if you let me go now."

Malenko didn't flinch at her threat. He stood frozen, still glaring at her. "Aren't you the least bit curious how I know so much about you?" he asked, clearly enjoying his cat-and-mouse game.

She smiled back at him. "I'm sure you'll be telling the police all that information when they come for you. They'll just tack on breaking and entering to murder."

It was disturbing how much information he had on her, but she was sure that Steven Selby could have dug up anything he wanted on her through his FBI connections. It wasn't difficult locating information on anyone nowadays.

"I don't think you have any kind of black magic powers. Steven Selby could have supplied you with any little obscure fact you might have wanted about me."

"Enough!" Conrad Malenko shrieked. He lurched forward, coming just short of where Brenda could get at him. His face twisted with such rage that it looked like a demonic mask. "This is how I see, Brenda," he hissed. "This is how I saw you, your house, your ghosts, your soul and your dreams."

From his forehead, flesh parted and another eye, bulging with red veins, glared down at her. A third eye! She stared in equal parts awe and distrust. Was this another silly Halloween trick or had Conrad Malenko developed the mystical, all-seeing Third Eye?

"Look at me, Brenda. I can swat you away with the wave of my hand." He backed away, blinking all three of his eyes. "But it is not you that I want."

His remark snaked away into the cold shadows, leaving a chill inside her soul. She had to keep talking, get him angry enough to trip up.

"I had part of your manuscript translated," she began. "I know the insane idea you have and what you need to achieve it. I won't be your next victim." She stared at him.

Malenko closed his third eye, and after a moment, it blended into the creases of his forehead and disappeared. "The ritual for eternal life is the most powerful and damning ritual in the black arts. You are invoking the Baphomet Goat, mother whore and bastard of darkness, purveyors of evil." He stopped and grinned at Brenda. Was it her imagination or were his eyes glowing? "Are you frightened, Brenda?"

Was he serious? Brenda didn't frighten so easily. Yes, there was a malignant air that clung to Malenko, but that wasn't what was bothering her. The intensity with which he believed what he was saying was far more frightening than her believing he had the power to attain immortality. A man with motivations such as his was capable of doing anything to attain it.

"I don't believe in eternal life," she said calmly, staring him down with her own steely gaze.

"Well, you should," he said matter-of-factly, "because you will live to become my adversary through time. Because, Brenda, we are light and dark. One chases after the other. We have traveled and will travel together, and that is why I cannot harm you . . ." The smile that almost cracked his flaky skin frightened her even more. "But I will take something that is yours, Brenda Strange. Something you love."

All the air rushed out of Brenda. She felt lightheaded. Desperate, she struggled in her chair against the handcuffs and rope at her feet. She didn't like the sound of his threat. "No."

He laughed. "Don't fret so, Brenda. You'll be leaving here soon, unharmed. You'll be back at Malfour with your companions from the other side and I will have eternity."

Just like that, he dismissed her. He turned away, melting into one of the shadowed corners.

"You can take her back home, now." His voice echoed in the room. Brenda couldn't see behind her. Was there someone there? She hadn't heard anyone come in.

"I won't let you murder any more innocent people!" she screamed into the darkness. "I know we didn't leave the Tides. I'll find out where you are and stop you."

Malenko said nothing. Was he still lurking in the shadows?

Just then, the two brutes appeared. Arthur Clemens wasn't with them. The blindfold was wrapped around her eyes again and tape stuck across her mouth. They lifted her from the chair, untied the rope binding her feet and took her away. Brenda didn't hear another sound from Conrad Malenko. Once again she struggled, but they were holding her so tightly, she knew she'd have bruises on her arms.

She tried to stay alert to sounds and smells that might give her a clue where she was but couldn't catch anything useful. The one thing she did know was that they'd gone up in an elevator and now were going back down.

She knew she was outside by the brisk air that slapped her face. It felt good after being cooped up in that hellish room. She was summarily shoved back into the car. The only one missing was Arthur Clemens. Was he there or had he stayed behind with Conrad Malenko?

It wasn't long before the car stopped. The ride from Malfour had been much longer. Brenda was betting that they'd ridden around in circles just to throw her off, in case she was damn good at judging distances, but hadn't bothered to confuse her on the return trip home.

She heard one car door open and then her door. Her legs were grabbed and roped together again. Another car door slammed. Had they taken her back to Malfour? Could she believe Conrad

Malenko, bona fide madman, when he assured her she would be returned safely back home? Maybe she was the mad one, thinking she could trust him.

One brute grabbed her feet as the other wrapped his arms beneath hers, and she was dragged from the car. By the way she was being lugged around, Brenda guessed they were going up stairs. Malfour's steps? She heard a door open and then she smelled Malfour. She was home. And the ghosts were in her head.

"We were afraid for your life, Brenda!" Carlotta sounded out of breath.

"Carlotta went hysterical, Brenda," Angelique teased.

"Please don't leave like that again."

"Where are they taking me?" Brenda asked silently.

"Upstairs."

She had guessed as much, by the angle she was being carried between the two men.

"They're heading to your bedroom," Carlotta said.

They traveled only a few feet more and then lifted her higher into the air and flung onto her bed. Well, she figured it had to be her bed. It was a nice soft landing.

"The keys are on your dresser. See how long it takes you to find them." The male voice was deep and young. Both of them laughed as their footsteps echoed away. Then the silence was complete.

"They're gone, Brenda," Angelique and Carlotta said almost in unison.

"You know, I wish you two could be more helpful than just telling me what I already know," Brenda responded telepathically. She struggled against the cuffs, but there was no way she was going to slip her hands through them, not unless she wanted to break her bones doing it.

She swung around to the edge of the bed and balanced herself on the floor. She would have to bunny-hop to the dresser. She knew the room from corner to corner, so that wouldn't be a problem.

She could imagine what she must have looked like, all five feet nine of her, hopping around with duct tape on her mouth, blindfolded, handcuffed and roped like a heifer. Brenda almost ran into the sharp edge of her late Victorian mahogany dresser. She spun around to reach atop the dresser and fumbled only a few minutes before she felt the keys.

It was going to be trickier getting both her cuffed hands coordinated enough to get the key into the lock. She took a deep breath, tried concentrating on a calm and soothing thought. She pictured herself and Tina in bed, snuggled together on a cold morning. That did the trick. Focusing on the key in one hand, Brenda guided it where she assumed the lock was. It didn't work.

She couldn't allow herself to get frustrated or she'd never uncuff herself. She didn't want to start all over again. She had the key in her hand and she was bound and determined to not lose it.

Being extra careful not to drop it, Brenda maneuvered the small key between her thumb and forefinger, carefully trailing the key along the metal cuffs until the tip slid into the lock. The cuffs were off in seconds, then the blindfold. Brenda rubbed at her wrists. They were sore, with narrow red welts where metal had bit into her skin.

She gently peeled the duct tape from her face. "Ouch. Son of a bitch, that hurt," she said aloud. Her feet were next.

She had to get to the phone and call Detective Reccio at the Monroe County Sheriff's Office and then Lisa Chambliss at the Tampa Police Department. Brenda had gone through the whole kidnapping in her head, paying particular attention to the ride to and from Conrad Malenko's room of red. She was convinced they had never left the Tides.

She looked at her clock radio. It was almost eleven. She'd left Strange Investigations at about nine thirty and taken roughly fifteen minutes or so to get home. So between her kidnapping, confrontation with Malenko and the ride back home, barely more than an hour had passed.

Brenda ran downstairs for her bag, which she found upended on the floor, the contents spilled out and scattered. She picked up the cell phone, where Detective Reccio's number was stored, and waited as it rang. She couldn't control the sense of urgency pent up inside her. It was like a spreading fire ready to burst out of control.

Reccio answered.

"Detective Reccio, this is Brenda Strange in Tampa." She didn't wait for him. "Please listen to me before interrupting. I know where Agent Selby and the Malenko manuscript are. I was kidnapped by Conrad Malenko. He has the manuscript. Steven Selby is some kind of double agent or something. He's working for Malenko. Selby was looking for the manuscript all along so he could deliver it to Malenko."

"Stop, Brenda," Reccio demanded. "Slow down." He paused.

"I know this sounds crazy, detective," she persisted, "but I think Malenko is a total maniac and intends to conduct some kind of black magic ritual using human heads. That's why Clifford Satterly and Hilda Moran were decapitated."

"Okay, suppose I believe you? What do you want me to do? And if you were kidnapped, how come you're on the phone talking to me?"

"This maniac was just playing a game. He let me go." Brenda shook her head in frustration, pushing back stray hairs from her face. "Look, I don't know why he kidnapped me. He's a lunatic. They don't need reasons to do things. Maybe he wanted to gloat about his grand plans. Some of his men were in my house, waiting for me when I got home. They handcuffed me, blindfolded and gagged me, then took me to Conrad Malenko's godforsaken hideout. They tried to fool me by riding around, but I know we didn't go very far from my house."

"How do you know that?"

"Because I know the roads around here so well I could drive them in my sleep. The old bridge that leads into and out of the Tides is built with pieced-together slabs of concrete. They've shifted with time and it makes for a bumpy ride no matter what car you're in. We didn't go over that bridge, detective. Malenko is here in the Tides—in my neighborhood—and I think I know exactly where. I can lead you to him."

There was only silence on the other end. Brenda grew even more impatient. Didn't Reccio want Malenko? He'd murdered Clifford Satterly, Hilda Moran and probably Jim Varley.

"Brenda, I can't just dispatch detectives to Tampa on your hunch. Now, you might very well be a great private investigator and maybe you're right about Malenko's whereabouts, but unless you have an address and proof positive he was the one who kidnapped you, I can't help you."

She snapped, "You're just going to wait until he takes someone else's head, then?"

"Just following protocol."

Brenda straightened up, took a deep breath and tried to continue without anger getting in the way. "Detective, there is one thing you might be able to help me with. Was Jim Varley decapitated?"

"You know I can't tell you that."

"I wouldn't ask if it wasn't important. Whether you like it or not, detective, I'm involved with this case. You know it."

After a long pause, Detective Reccio sighed. "Yeah, he was. And we still haven't found either of the heads."

Chapter Fifteen

Malenko needed five heads, one for each point of the inverted pentagram. Clifford, Hilda and Varley added up to only three. Brenda shivered, unable to control the shakes that followed. Was Malenko making plans at this moment to murder two more people? Could one of them be her? Then her heart started thumping rapidly. What if it was Tina he was after?

Brenda had to stop him, but she couldn't do it alone. She needed help from the police. Monroe County wasn't going to play the part of the triumphant cavalry to the rescue. That left Lisa Chambliss and the Tampa Police Department. But she knew Lisa would just echo Reccio's objections. The police needed something concrete. They weren't going to go out on a limb based on Brenda's ideas. So she had to find out where Malenko was.

She still suspected he was the one who'd purchased Stewart and Joan's old mansion. "Brad Smith" could be an alias. A name used to hide him wherever he went. He was the mysterious stranger with the huge moving vans. His black limousine was the one scouting out Malfour that day she nearly ran into it. And he was the figure in her backyard that rainy afternoon.

Brenda hastened into the library where the laptop sat on the desk. She signed online and did a Google search for Carriage Movers. Her wrists still stung from the handcuffs. She found only one exact hit for the company. They were in New York.

"Bingo," she said aloud. The Web site wasn't much, but it did list an address and phone number.

"Brenda, stop, please. Don't get any further involved." Carlotta sounded frightened.

Brenda shrugged her off. "I can't listen to you right now."

"There is much evil and power surrounding this. You mustn't chase after this man."

"He came after me, Carlotta. I can't back out." Malenko's threat still echoed in Brenda's head. "He's a danger to all of us. I have to stop him."

"Let someone else do it, then," Angelique chimed in.

Brenda stopped in midkeystroke. "What a brilliant idea." She reached for the phone and punched in Kevin O'Connor's number in New Jersey.

"What are you doing?" both Carlotta and Angelique asked.

"I helped Kevin out with the Paula Drakes case. He can do me a return favor now by checking out Carriage Movers in New York and hopefully get proof that Malenko used them to move to the Tides and Stewart's old place."

"Kevin O'Connor Private Investigations."

His voice made Brenda smile. It felt good. "So you're answering your own phone now? What's the matter, your staff took Saturday off?"

"Hey, B.S. Always great to hear from you." He paused. "Wait a minute, are you calling 'cause I still haven't cut you a check for the Paula Drakes case?"

"No, no. I didn't bill you. That was a favor."

"Uh-oh, that means I owe you one and this is it, right?"

"Kevin, you're a great PI. I'm glad I learned from the best."

"You were a great learner. I'm almost afraid to ask what you got going. I don't do spooks or zombies or anything like that, you know."

"No zombies or spooks. I need you to dig into the records of a moving company called Carriage Movers in New York."

"What kind of info do you need me to get?"

"I've got an address and several names. If Carriage Movers made the move, I'll need records. Hard-copy validation. Fax it to me ASAP."

"I'll check them out myself." There was silence for a moment. "B.S., you okay?"

"It's important that I get this information, Kevin. It could be a missing piece to a puzzle I've got to complete. You know how it goes. You've been in the business longer than I have."

"Sure. Give me what you've got."

Brenda gave him everything—the Davis address, the names of Conrad Malenko, BC Corporation, Baphomet Chosen, Arthur Clemens, Steven Selby and Brad Smith. She didn't think Conrad Malenko would openly use his name. If Brad Smith wasn't Conrad Malenko, she could at least find out where Brad Smith came from. Equipped with that information, she could proceed to find out who he was. She had to start with something.

Before she went to see Lisa Chambliss, she had to call Tina and warn her not to come home yet. With the dangers developing here, maybe Tina shouldn't come at all for spring break. It would break Brenda's heart to have to wait until school finished up in May to see Tina, but she'd rather have her safe than have to worry about her here. Brenda was seriously considering just boarding a plane and heading up to Tina instead.

The apartment phone in Jersey rang and rang. No answer. Brenda tried Tina's cell phone. She got the recording.

"Where the hell are you? Answer the phone," Brenda whispered to herself. Her lover didn't answer. It was Saturday, Tina should have been home. Brenda reluctantly left a message, making sure Tina knew it was urgent.

From out of the corner of her eye, Brenda caught a furry movement under one of the library chairs. Butterscotch peeked out, then rushed over to wrap himself around her legs, meowing as he looked at her with grateful eyes. He always brought joy to heart.

She scooped him up, hugged him tight and kissed the top of his tiny head. "Oh, baby, you must have been so scared with those nasty men in here." He squirmed out of her arms and flicked his tail at her. "C'mon, Butterscotch, I've got to get changed."

He followed her up the stairs and into her bedroom. She had to change clothes. She felt dirty. Violated. She couldn't stand that they had touched her skin.

After a quick shower, Brenda slipped into a camel-colored skirt, black turtleneck pullover and black ankle boots. She gave her hair a quick brushing and rushed back down the stairs. Should she call TPD headquarters to see if Lisa was on duty? Maybe she was out working a case.

Brenda opted to head over without calling first, but not before slipping her Walther PPK into the black belt holster underneath her pullover.

She would have wanted to question Tony on her way out, but he wasn't on duty. She sped past the guardhouse. On the way down the Causeway, she decided to ring Cubbie. Not so much because she'd promised to, but because she needed to know that Cubbie was okay. Malenko's threat was still fresh in her head.

She had a hard time explaining to Cubbie what she was doing out on the road again and not home in bed. Brenda wasn't about to bring Cubbie into this situation, so she assured her she was okay and that she'd see her on Monday. Anything to put Cubbie at ease.

Lisa Chambliss met Brenda in the lobby of the big blue Tampa Police Department building. She was on her way out to follow up on one of her cases. Detective Chambliss was Brenda's "in" at

TPD. Not all detectives or police officers took kindly to private investigators, and few would go out of their way to even throw a bone to a PI, but Lisa had been a long-time link to the law in Tampa for Kevin's Jersey PI office. Brenda was thankful he had hooked her and Lisa up for the Paula Drakes case.

Lisa greeted Brenda with a big smile. Brenda could never quite put a finger on what she found attractive about Lisa Chambliss's smile. It made the pixie-like face light up.

"Brenda Strange." Lisa stopped and looked Brenda over. "You seem pretty worked up. What kind of horror movie case are you working this time?"

"One that has me uncomfortable. I wouldn't ask if I didn't need your help."

Her smile fading, Lisa studied Brenda's face. "Okay, sounds serious. I'll help if I can."

"I was hired by a client who was murdered two days after I talked to him. He wanted me to find a rare handwritten manuscript that he said was stolen from him. To keep a very long and complex story short, I got the manuscript dumped in my lap, lost it, two more people have been beheaded—"

"Wait a minute," Lisa interrupted. "Beheaded?"

Brenda nodded. "The manuscript is a book of the black arts— in particular, a ritual to attain eternal life." The look on Lisa's face stopped her. She didn't want to exasperate Lisa with her strange cases. She knew Lisa didn't go for the supernatural or the weird. But Brenda needed her to listen. "Please, Lisa, don't tune me out yet."

Lisa shook her head. "Brenda, maybe you should be some kind of ghost hunter or something instead of a PI. I've never met one with your caseload."

"Lisa, I was kidnapped," Brenda blurted out. She was getting frustrated. Her insides were so tensed up she wanted to throw up. Pain shot through her body. Finally, she rolled up the sleeves of her pullover and showed Lisa her wrists. "I was handcuffed, blindfolded and taken to the house of the man who wrote that manuscript."

Lisa reached out and grabbed both of her hands, her face showing surprise and concern. "PI work is dangerous." She studied the fading red marks on Brenda's wrists, and then focused her dark eyes back on Brenda's face. "Tell me more about what happened." She held on to Brenda's hands.

Brenda felt uncomfortable and pulled away. "The manuscript was written in longhand and in Russian by Conrad Malenko, some kind of megalomaniac who dabbled in black magic and consorted with Hitler during World War Two—"

"He's still alive?"

"He looks like a walking mummy, but very much alive. I had parts of Malenko's manuscript translated and apparently it's a blueprint for making some sort of deal with a demon for eternal life."

Lisa was slowly shaking her head. "Brenda, these Satanists are always more bark than bite."

"They're not Satanists," Brenda said. "Malenko is behind a very powerful worldwide organization that is using a major international corporation as a front for his crazy quest." She sighed. "Malenko's ritual calls for the heads of five people, one for each point of the inverted pentagram. He has already murdered three people, all of them beheaded."

Lisa held Brenda's stare. "You realize this sounds like some B movie, don't you."

"He threatened to take something from me, Lisa. Something I love, he said." The words and their ramifications still turned Brenda's insides to ice.

"And you believe this guy?" Lisa asked, her disbelief evident.

"I wouldn't be here if I didn't."

Lisa put her hands up and shook her head. "I don't know what I can do to help, Brenda." She glanced back at Brenda's hands. "Did you get a plate number on the car? An address to this Conrad Malenko's house. Anything?"

Brenda just stared into Lisa dark eyes. The detective clearly wanted to believe. Wanted to help. Whether she believed in psychic powers or not, she was sending out some very strong signals. Apparently, Brenda wasn't adept enough at convincing her.

Brenda shied away from Lisa's gaze, looking down at the floor. It needed mopping. "I know where he is."

"You have an address?"

"I think he moved into Stewart Davis's old mansion."

Lisa opened her mouth to say something but didn't.

"I know it isn't enough. I'm sorry I can't give you more, Lisa, but I know in my gut that this man is dangerous and he means to harm me in some way or someone close to me."

Unexpectedly, Lisa reached out for Brenda's arm. "I don't know what you expect me to do, Brenda. I can't help you if you don't have a case. You have no solid evidence or information. I believe you were kidnapped and I worry about you, but there's nothing I can do unless you can bring me something I can work with."

Brenda didn't pull away from Lisa's touch this time. She'd expected this outcome of her conversation with Lisa. Her options were dwindling. It was time to take action, with or without Lisa and the TPD.

"I'll get you an address and more." Now Brenda pulled away.

Lisa yanked her back. "I'm going to put you on the Neighbor House Watch patrol. We've got a couple of officers who make the rounds of homes where the residents might be away for long periods and request we keep an eye on the properties for them. I'm sending an officer to the Tides to keep a watch on Malfour and on you."

Brenda didn't think that would make much difference but wasn't about to turn down Lisa's attempt to help. She mustered a smile. "Thanks, but make sure they don't get in my way."

She left, relishing the look of surprise on Lisa's face.

Chapter Sixteen

Brenda had her cell phone, packages of muffins, grapes, a bottle of water, her best Minolta binoculars and her 9mm Walther PPK. She'd also loaded her old Nikon 35mm, complete with telephoto lens, with high-speed black-and-white film. She rented a dark green Jeep SUV and found a thick clump of trees about a hundred yards from the old Davis mansion. Brenda thought she'd prepared well for her stakeout. She'd even smudged some dark eye shadow all over her face to blend in with the dark interior of the car. Otherwise, her white complexion would stick out like an unwanted beacon in the twilight.

After getting home from the police department, Brenda had made sure Butterscotch's food dish was full, checked her messages and set out for the stakeout. She was glad it was the weekend. Brenda didn't think she could stand up to Cubbie's searching eyes with a lie.

Tina hadn't called, but at least Brenda got a chance for a quick phone call to her dad. She needed reassurance that all her loved ones were doing well, that they were safe. Tina had her worried. If she didn't hear from her by tomorrow, Brenda was going to call the art institute where Tina worked. Or her parents.

The old Davis house had developed an air of malignancy. The bright, rich colors and lights that Stewart and Joan had showcased in their home had been replaced by a dark, lifeless husk. Was Conrad Malenko living there? If not, then who was? Brad Smith? And who was he? Brenda had been tempted to merely march up to the door, knock and barge her way in, steamrolling anyone who offered resistance. But what if those two big brutes of Malenko's answered her knock? What then?

No, a stakeout was the most efficient way to get the information she needed for Lisa at TPD. Lisa wouldn't be able to refute photographic proof. Brenda wanted a search warrant and in order to get one, she needed solid evidence. Malenko was there. She felt it in her bones. And the manuscript was there too. A thought that chilled Brenda even more than Malenko seeped in her veins. What if the heads were in there somewhere? Hilda's, Clifford's and Varley's.

Brenda shook off the gruesome thought and pulled out the binoculars.

The Davis house stood like a mausoleum, silent and devoid of activity. Until 2:25 a.m. Brenda had all but lost hope that she was going to get anything tonight. She started counting the number of opossums that scurried about, rummaging through the bushes and crossing to and from the house. They reminded her of giant rats.

Then she heard the quiet, throaty sound of a new car. She ducked down more out of instinct than fear of being spotted. Unless they suspected her presence, she was in a good spot. Brenda grabbed the binoculars again. At the front porch of the large man-

137

sion, a small light erupted. It was dim, with barely enough power to illuminate the circular drive where the car had parked, but enough for Brenda to see two big men emerge from the vehicle.

They looked like football players, bulging muscles protruding through the turtleneck sweaters they wore. Were they the brutes who'd kidnapped her? She fumbled in the dark for the camera. She knew she was far enough away so that the sound of the shutter wouldn't alert them to her position.

Each man took a big black box out of the car, handling them in almost slow motion, as if the boxes might contain nitro or explosives and shouldn't be dropped. Brenda clicked away. What the hell could be in those boxes? One of the men pulled a card out of his back pocket and flashed it in front of the door, which opened electronically. Both men disappeared inside. She took a couple of more shots.

She couldn't contain a low whistle. Wow, she thought, Malenko had made Stewart's old house into a fortress. It was obvious he wanted to keep prying eyes out and had done some very extensive and expensive renovations to the mansion. He could, she thought, very easily have installed an elevator and converted the upstairs into a makeshift pyramid for his insane black magic rituals.

Brenda stiffened as one of the men came back out to the car. He pulled out another box and then disappeared back into the house, the door closing shut behind him.

Oh, my God, Brenda thought. There were three boxes. What if the heads of Hilda, Clifford and Varley were in those boxes? Could Malenko be ready to initiate his ritual? But if the manuscript translation was right, he needed five heads, one for each point of the pentagram. Malenko was still missing two heads.

The light at the front of the house blinked out. Again, she was left in total darkness, with only the light of the silver half moon in the star-studded sky above. Brenda stayed, feeling comfortable in the cocoon of the black night, and waited.

ᏇᎯᎶ

Nancy Alexandra Strange diary, October 16, 1977

Raymond is still having a hard time understanding why I won't allow Brenda to visit Grandmama. He doesn't know about the Winters women and the matriarchal society they are guardians of. Poor Raymond never did push me about my refusal to attend church services or my aversion to religious groups and activities. It must be hard for him to be married to such a bitch like me. I admit I'm a difficult woman to live with, but Grandmama made me what I am. When the matriarchs discovered I had none of the Winters psychic gifts, I was shoved aside. I never once was invited to their monthly meetings. Those mysterious meetings only the Winters women attended. Only they knew the location where the meetings were held, and all of them went, even the little girls. All the ones with the gift, that is.

It was hell to face up to Grandmama at first. She demanded I bring Brenda to her for a visit once a month. Yeah, I knew what that visit entailed. She wanted Brenda to be initiated into their little circle. Well, I won't allow it. Grandmama says I'm blinding Brenda. Without proper exercise and training, Brenda's powers will shrivel and become dormant. She will be blind like me. Like me. I enjoyed slapping my mother. She wasn't my mother anymore. She was just an old witch and Brenda was my daughter. She will not have her.

Poor Raymond. He doesn't understand.

Brenda woke up to a buzzing sound. She moaned, trying to get the early-morning fog from her thoughts, and stumbled out of bed, nearly rolling over Butterscotch. She went to the bedroom window, where the buzzing sound grew into the familiar sound of a lawnmower.

From the second-story window, Carlos, the yard man, appeared like a windup toy, riding his lawnmower in wide circles around her perennial garden and trees. She'd almost forgotten that Carlos, who'd been doing the Malfour lawn since Brenda and Tina bought the house, came twice a month. Always on Sunday.

The sun was bright and the wind ruffled the long palm fronds like flags flapping against the blue sky. It seemed so much like a normal Sunday morning. The beginnings of a perfect day. But the gun on her dresser and the film canister next to it were jarring reminders that this was anything but an ordinary March Sunday.

Brenda checked the clock radio. It was ten a.m. She'd spent time on Saturday reading more of her mother's diary and found answers to questions that had always haunted her. Her grandmother had been a taboo subject in the Strange household. Brenda never got to know her. She remembered catching words here and there from whispered arguments between her mother and father, but that was it.

What Brenda wanted to do today was examine the pictures from last night's stakeout. But first, she had to find a photo lab that would print the black-and-white film without having to send it out. Most one-hour labs were equipped for color processing. You had to wait days for black-and-white. Brenda headed for the shower. She was desperate for a nice, hot shower. Yesterday had been a long day. She just wanted to wash it all away.

Brenda had barely removed her pajama bottoms when the sound of the fax machine downstairs sent her running to the library, only a towel wrapped around herself. A stream of papers spewed slowly from the fax. They were receipts from Carriage Movers in New York.

"Thank you, thank you, Kevin," Brenda said out loud as the last page came to a stop. She scooped up the three pages and started back upstairs to the shower. One quick look at the faxes brought only disappointment.

The copies were receipts and item description forms for a move Carriage Movers made to 102 Peppertree Lane. The Davis mansion. Brenda took the papers with her into the bathroom as she looked desperately for some kind of signature. They were all signed by Brad Smith. The faxes were useless without a name Brenda could connect to Conrad Malenko. Yes, she could point out that someone by the name of Brad Smith hired Carriage Movers to move them into the Davis mansion, but that was all. It wasn't enough for Lisa Chambliss. Brenda could hear her objections now.

Brenda savored her hot shower, put on a sweatshirt and jeans and grabbed the faxed receipts from Carriage Movers. After a breakfast of eggs over medium and toast, she started out to Bob Baggett Photography. Not only did they specialize in black-and-white photography, but they were also willing to process the film for her on Sunday. For a hefty rush fee. Brenda didn't mind paying the double high cost of processing high-speed film and quick turn-around. The pictures would be ready by noon.

Chapter Seventeen

Later that afternoon, Detective Lisa Chambliss sat back in the chair, her arms crossed, and stared at Brenda. Brenda had invited her to the Space Age Café, a quaint coffee shop in Hyde Park that used classic science fiction films and television as its inspiration for décor. It wasn't far from Strange Investigations and Tina's gallery. The big TV screen flickered with images of Stanley Kubrik's *2001: A Space Odyssey*. Keir Dullea was in deep conversation with Gary Lockwood, trying in vain to keep their words secret from the ship's computer, HAL.

"You knew what I was going to say about these, right?" Lisa pointed at the stack of photos of two men lugging boxes from a dark car. The faxed copies of inventory from Carriage Movers in New York lay beside them.

Yes, Brenda expected that Lisa would consider them worthless. There was nothing there that Lisa or any other detective could use to get a search warrant. Nothing. But Brenda had to try. Desperation was setting in.

"Can you run a check on this Brad Smith?" Brenda edged up to the table. "It's an alias or a fake name, I'm sure of it. You have the resources to do that, Lisa. Maybe the name can be linked back to BC Corporation or even to Malenko himself."

Lisa took a swallow from the coffee mug in front of her, then sighed. "Brenda, I can guarantee you're not going to take my advice, but you're going to get it anyway. Go home. Make sure you have your security system activated. Let my officers watch your house and the neighborhood . . ." She shrugged. "Let me take care of the situation."

Brenda didn't answer right away. She didn't quite know what to make of the comment. Was she offering personal protection for Brenda? Why? Did Lisa believe her but couldn't come right out and say so? Brenda couldn't put her own safety in someone else's hands, let alone the safety of her loved ones.

She shook her head, exhausted. "I appreciate your concern, but I was kidnapped yesterday, Lisa. Bound, gagged, removed from my house against my will and threatened. I can't afford to take my eyes off this and hand over responsibility for what might happen."

"I'm not just someone else, Brenda. I'm a cop. I'm trained for this type of situation."

Saddened, Brenda lowered her head, unable to suppress a frown. "What situation? According to you, there is no situation."

Lisa put up her hands to object. "Don't mangle my intentions."

"I'm grateful for everything you've done to help me, but I'm on my own on this one." Brenda pulled out a ten-dollar bill and left it on the table under her coffee mug. "Thanks for meeting me, Lisa." She started to collect the photos and faxes, but Lisa grabbed her hand.

"Let me take those."

Brenda stopped and looked at her in surprise.

"Don't look so damned shocked." Lisa gathered up the photos and papers and tucked them in her jacket. "I might be able to track something down."

✧

Brenda was barely out of the Space Age Café before she was on the phone trying to reach Tina again. As the phone rang and rang, the beating in Brenda's chest grew louder and harder. Where was Tina?

Brenda pulled into the front parking space of the Marchanti Gallery of Fine Sculpture. Tina's new gallery. As she stared at the beautiful storefront with the custom-made canopy, Brenda couldn't suppress the tears. The gallery was empty without Tina, just as was Brenda's life. She needed her lover more than ever. Brenda wiped her eyes with the back of her hand and was about to try calling Tina's dean at the school, when the cell phone chirped. It wasn't a Tampa area code and it wasn't Tina.

"Hello, this is Brenda Strange."

"Ms. Strange, it's Matt Ritter."

"Matt, is everything okay?" It was her first concern.

"Everything is better than okay." He hesitated. "I just thought, since you were so helpful to me and my mom, that you should know what's going on." He paused again. "My Aunt Hilda's lawyer contacted us. She left me her entire estate, including her autograph business and inventory. Well, she also left some money to my mom."

Brenda had been right. Hilda Moran had loved her nephew deeply. "Your aunt made sure you were taken care of, Matt. Consider yourself a lucky young man. I don't imagine you'll have any financial problems with college now."

"No, ma'am. As a matter of fact, I'm going to decide on the college me and my Aunt Hilda were filling out the papers for that . . . that"—he fumbled for words—"that day I found her." The last sentence was whispered.

Brenda's curiosity was piqued. "Matt, I appreciate you calling me. I was concerned about you and your mom. Have the police spoken to either of you?"

"Yes, ma'am. Both me and my mom told everything we know to the two detectives who came from the Monroe County Sheriff's Office."

"Was it Detective Reccio?"

Matt didn't hesitate. "Yes, ma'am, he was one of them."

Brenda wished both Matt and Heather well. Although both of them had much to gain from Hilda Moran's death, they hadn't murdered her.

She disconnected with Matt and punched in the directory in the cell phone. Controlling the desperation threatening to choke her, Brenda decided to call Marsha Koenig, the dean at the Art Institute and Tina's boss. Tina had added her number to Brenda's cell phone in case of an emergency. This was close enough to one.

As Brenda listened to the ringing on the other end, she revved up the Jag and continued up Swan Avenue toward Bayshore. She knew it wasn't a good idea to talk and drive at the same time, but she made sure she drove carefully.

Marsha was home. She was friendly, but Brenda just wanted to know about Tina.

"No, I don't know where she is," Marsha said.

"I can't get hold of her. It's important and I'm a bit worried." Brenda wasn't going to explain anything to Marsha Koening. "I know she wanted to request some days before spring break to come home early. Did she talk to you about that?"

The silence on the other end of the phone disturbed her. Something was wrong. Marsha wasn't telling her the truth.

"Marsha, is everything okay? I need to talk to Tina right away." *Tell me where she is, damn it!* Brenda felt the blood pumping through her veins heat up and the ringing grew loud in her ears.

At last Marsha said, "Please don't tell Tina I finked her out. She wanted to surprise you. We gave her the days off she wanted plus some, but not before working her hard. She's been running around like crazy getting her sculptures ready. She booked an early flight to Tampa."

Brenda's brain was still clicking, but she couldn't think. She opened her mouth once, but nothing came out. She tried again. "Tina is coming here?"

Marsha sounded cautious. "She didn't want you to know. It was

145

supposed to be a surprise." She paused. "Maybe her flight got held up."

"When did she leave?"

"I think it was an early bird this morning."

Brenda's insides went cold. It was nearly three o'clock. She swallowed hard, trying to keep down the bile burning its way up. News of Tina's surprise visit should have brought ecstatic joy but instead, fear was gnawing through her. She didn't know why she was reacting this way.

Brenda disconnected without another word to Marsha Koenig. She had just turned into the Tides and approached the guard-house. She wished she didn't have to stop. She wanted to speed on through. Get home to Malfour. Would Tina be waiting there for her?

It was a different security guard and not Tony Cutcheon, so she had to stop. After flashing her resident card, she gunned the Jag and sped over the bridge. Was Tina home already?

"Please be home, baby, please be home," Brenda repeated to herself. She took the sharp right turn onto Sea Breeze Lane too fast and nearly spun out. As soon as Brenda set eyes on the loom-ing Victorian she called Malfour House, her heart sank. She knew Tina wasn't there. It was a dead house.

Brenda screeched the car to a stop, ran into the house and found chaos in the foyer. Two large open suitcases and a smaller carrying case were sprawled on the floor, and clothes lay crumpled in piles. Tina's clothes.

"Dear God, no." The whisper escaped as she furiously started to gather up the clothes and put them back into the suitcases. "Tina," she called out into the empty house. "Tina, damn it, are you here?" She dropped the clothes and started up the stairs. "Angelique! Carlotta!"

Brenda got to the top of the second floor and stopped. Both Angelique and Carlotta stood side by side in front of Tina's work-room, the ghostly gray of their faces dark and somber.

"What the hell is going on here? Where is Tina?" Brenda was shaking with fear, her voice on the edge of breaking.

The dark shadows that had threatened to overtake the Malfour walls suddenly seemed to come alive and ooze toward Tina's room! They were guiding Brenda there. She was suddenly terrified. Standing here in her own home, confronted by two ghosts and inexplicable dark forms on her walls, she experienced a deep fear of what might be waiting for her behind that door.

She took one hesitant step, then barged into the room that Tina used for her sculptures and supplies. When Susan Christie had been at Malfour last December investigating its two haunts, Angelique and Carlotta, the stains in Tina's room had begun to take form. Weeks ago, Brenda had noticed that they were taking on a more distinct shape. It was now a complete head, the fingers of black stains appearing like a charcoal drawing of Tina.

Brenda's knees almost buckled. She leaned against the door for support. The shadows had all united to make one giant head that looked as similar to Tina's as any artist's rendering. The buzzing in Brenda's ear turned into Carlotta's voice.

"They took her, Brenda. Those men took Tina."

Brenda shook her head, waved Carlotta off. "No. This can't be happening."

"You have to go find her, Brenda," Angelique said.

The room suddenly began to spin and Brenda found it hard to breathe. She stumbled back out into the hall, hugging the wall. "How long ago . . ." She paused, finding her thoughts jumbled. She couldn't think straight. "When did Tina get here?"

"Shortly after you left," Carlotta said. "They were waiting for her, Brenda."

"They're like ghosts. They have the power to open locked doors," Angelique added.

"Malenko," Brenda said slowly. "He has the power."

"He is evil incarnate," Carlotta said. "Do not go after him, Brenda. Call the police. Let them find Tina."

Brenda shushed her. "To hell with the police. I know where Tina is and I'm going for her."

Brenda walked into her room and grabbed extra bullets for her Walther PPK. No longer afraid, but determined and outraged, she stuffed them in her jacket pockets. Powerful magician or not, she'd like to see him stop nine-millimeter bullets. Conrad Malenko was not going to harm Tina or anyone else Brenda loved. She'd use the gun if she had to.

She was on her way down the stairs, ready to break into the old Davis mansion, when her cell phone chirped. It was Tina's number displayed.

"Tina!" Brenda's heart jumped.

At first, there was silence. Then a man's voice said, "You missed her. But we didn't." The phone went dead.

"You son of a bitch." Brenda ran out the door. She knew that each minute wasted could mean Tina was in more danger. She struggled to keep the images of five heads in a pentagram from overcrowding her thoughts. She was damned if she'd let Tina's be one of those heads.

Chapter Eighteen

Brenda floored the Jag and started toward Tide Boulevard and Peppertree Lane. She pressed the button on her cell phone for Lisa Chambliss and waited. "Please, Lisa, answer your phone. Be there, please."

"Lisa Chambliss."

"Lisa, it's Brenda. Malenko's got Tina. I'm on my way to the old Davis house." Brenda disconnected. She didn't have the time to spar with Lisa on the phone. Within minutes, she was pulling up the circular drive at Stewart Davis's old house. This time, she didn't have to hide.

Brenda came to an abrupt stop, sending pebbles bouncing up against her car. The house was desolate. There wasn't a car in sight, although the limo could be in the adjacent garage. Was Tina inside? Jumping out of the Jag, she ran to the two double doors. They offered no resistance. They weren't locked. For a few seconds, she stood in what was once a lavish foyer decorated with the most expensive art objects and paintings. The foyer and huge sunken living room were, as far as Brenda could tell, empty. A film of dust coated the floor and there were small piles of Sheetrock, paint buckets and tools. The place was only a shell of its former self.

"Tina?" Brenda called out as she made her way through the unkempt house. She knew Malenko was there. This was where they'd brought her. All she had to do was find that elevator. She'd go through every floor in the house to find it.

As she moved through the house, the strong scent of gasoline hit her. It was splattered on the walls and some parts of the floor. She had to find Tina.

"Tina! Answer me," Brenda yelled even louder. She went from room to room. Each one was empty. They hadn't been lived in since both Stewart and Joan were gone. Obviously, Malenko had had his reasons for buying the mansion. Did he merely need a place to work his black magic?

She wound her way up the once elegant spiral staircase in the living room. The place was dense with dirt and dust. She didn't feel comfortable heading upstairs without protection. She pulled out her Walther PPK, held it in front of her with both hands on the grip and proceeded to the second floor.

"Tina!" she called into each empty room. At a short intersecting hallway, she spotted a narrow recessed door at the end that had been left slightly ajar. She crept toward it cautiously, her gun pointed outward. The door had been built flush with the wall. Like a hidden passage, it sported a tiny button at the very top. She slowly pulled the door back. It was the elevator!

She made sure there was no one inside. It was a large elevator. Why had Stewart built such a large elevator in his house? Or had Malenko built this when he moved in? He was frail and had difficulty walking. There was only an up arrow on a big red button in the elevator. Brenda pressed it.

Two slim silver doors whisked shut and the elevator began to ascend. The thumping in Brenda's chest was so intense she thought her heart was going to explode. Her skin tingled as if tiny needles were biting deep into her.

The elevator slowed, then stopped. Brenda raised her gun again. She would shoot anyone standing in her way. Except Tina, of course. The doors opened into blackness. It was an empty, darkened hallway, ending at a black door directly ahead of her. Only the dim elevator light cast an eerie glow. The place reminded her of underground bunkers she'd seen in World War II films.

"Tina? Are you there?" Brenda began the slow walk toward the door. She hesitated when she noticed it was cracked open. As she approached, she heard the sound of footsteps and what sounded like water splashing. Then the smell of gasoline stung her eyes and nose. Brenda ran into the room, her gun aimed and ready to shoot.

She found herself in that same red pyramid room where she'd been brought to meet Conrad Malenko. Except it was different and the smell in the room was rancid. It reeked of blood. And Steven Selby stood in a giant inverted pentagram in the center of the room, a large gasoline can in his hand.

"Hello, Ms. Strange. You're a bit late, I'm afraid." His grin was malevolent. He pointed to the gun in Brenda's hand. "You can put that down. I'm not armed. You wouldn't shoot an unarmed man, I know."

Brenda didn't lower the gun. "Where is Tina? I know she's here. I know you took her."

Selby turned his back on her and continued spilling gasoline all over the floor and walls. "I said you were late, Ms. Strange. I'm just finishing up my job here."

Brenda gazed around the room. There were dark pools of blood at each tip of the pentagram. The heads! Had Malenko accomplished his ritual? Dear God, Tina couldn't have been here! Brenda tightened her grip on the gun. "I'm going to ask you one more time, you son of a bitch, where is Tina?"

Selby stopped and turned again to Brenda. "Look, you made me lose my concentration and now I spilled some of this gasoline on my suit." He pointed to his tan slacks, where drops of gas had spattered. "You know, this stuff evaporates quickly, so I can't enjoy our little meeting for long." His stare bore into hers. "The party's over. Mr. Malenko asked me to offer his apologies that he couldn't invite you."

"You bastard, if you've harmed her, I'll kill you. I'll hunt down Malenko too."

Steven Selby chuckled. He began to inch closer to her.

"Stop it right there." Brenda waved the gun at him.

"Don't you want to know about Tina? She was very upset that you weren't going to make it to the gathering. She couldn't control herself. You could say she lost her head."

He started to laugh again, but Brenda lunged for him, grabbed him by the throat and jammed the gun into his belly. The smell of gasoline nearly made her gag.

"No, I don't believe you. Tina is here somewhere." She could have strangled him. Her whole body was shaking in rage. She couldn't believe Selby. She couldn't.

Selby just looked at her smugly. "I know you won't kill me in cold blood. Just let go of me."

She wanted to pull the trigger right now. Selby would die instantly. But what good would that do? He was her only hope of finding Tina. He would have to tell the truth to the police. She would just hold him here until Lisa Chambliss could arrive. She released him and backed off but kept the gun aimed at him.

"Don't even flinch or I *will* shoot you. You'll have to answer to the police, and then you'll have to answer to me."

Selby shook his head. "I don't think so. Even if I do stick around for your little game, do you think I won't be able to simply walk away from all this? I have enough means to escape even the most serious of situations I get myself into. I'm a chameleon agent, Ms. Strange. Your police will get all the facts I have about this case. I've been doing undercover work, you see. You'll come out looking like a little schoolgirl playing detective with the big boys."

He was probably the Brad Smith who had signed the Carriage

Movers contracts, Brenda thought. "You're Brad Smith, aren't you?"

He pulled out a match and held it out toward her, taunting her. "Too bad you won't find out."

"I know what you're trying to do, Selby. You're trying to erase the evidence. You can burn this fucking house down if that's what you want, but you're not getting away. Both of us are leaving alive."

Without hesitating, he flicked the match behind him, right into the center of the blood-soaked pentagram. The fire erupted in a whoosh of angry flames, big pillars of black smoke rising to the ceiling and swallowing the walls. The heat was blasting Brenda's face. She knew that if she lost her concentration on Selby, he was gone. She needed to grab him and get out now, while they still could.

"This entire house is drenched in gasoline. It's going down in minutes." Selby's voice was hoarse. He coughed.

Brenda could no longer see him. The smoke was rolling toward her, and between her and Selby a wall of flames was eating everything in its path.

"Selby!" She couldn't breathe.

Chapter Nineteen

"Brenda!" From somewhere out in the hall, Lisa Chambliss was calling her.

Brenda put her gun away and shielded her eyes from the fire. Selby was gone. But where and how? Was there a secret exit somewhere? She couldn't see anything and her throat was closing up. She could no longer swallow. She ran out of the room and headed for the elevator.

"Brenda. This way." Lisa Chambliss was at the elevator, holding it open.

Brenda could barely see her. Thank God for the elevator light. The flames were working their way out into the narrow hall. She thought the clothes on her back might be on fire. Her skin felt raw.

Lisa's strong hands grabbed her in a tight grip. "We've got to use the stairs. We couldn't find them. Do you know where they are?" She had a wet towel covering her mouth and nose.

Brenda stared at her for a few seconds, then remembered Tina.

She couldn't leave without Tina. She pulled away from Lisa. "I've got to get Tina."

Lisa held on tighter. "We've got to get out of here. The whole house is drenched in gasoline. The fire department is on its way. Tina isn't here. We've searched the whole house. Where are the stairs?"

Maybe the stairs were in that red room? Maybe that's how Selby got away? Brenda couldn't leave without searching for Tina herself. She couldn't leave without knowing what happened. She looked at Lisa. "You've got to help me find Tina."

"I'm not sticking around to be a piece of burnt bacon. Don't make me use force, Brenda, 'cause I'm not leaving without you. We've got to risk the elevator, then, but we're leaving now."

Brenda didn't put up a fight. Lisa pushed her into the elevator and punched the red button. The elevator doors closed too slowly. Brenda was afraid they would jam. It was a risk using the elevator, but as far as Brenda knew, there were no stairs.

"C'mon, damn it, close!" Lisa Chambliss kicked at the doors. They finally closed and Brenda felt the slight jerk as the elevator begin to move down. The pain was unbearable each time she tried to breathe, but at least she could swallow now. She didn't have the strength left to stand on her feet. She slumped slowly to the floor.

Lisa was immediately at her side. "Hey, are you okay? Can you breathe? Can you see me?"

Brenda looked up to see rivulets of sweat running down Lisa's face, her concern evident. "I'm okay."

The elevator stopped and the doors opened into a part of the Davis mansion Brenda wasn't familiar with, maybe a den or library, but she saw moving lights directly ahead of them. Flashlights. Three police officers came to Lisa's side. Behind them, a string of firefighters in heavy suits and masks were lugging big hoses and making their way through the house.

"The whole upstairs is engaged, detective. We've got to move fast. This way."

The smoke wasn't as thick as it had been upstairs, but the sound of crackling flames meant the fire was still raging. Through the stinging smoke, Brenda saw more firefighters hosing down the walls. She recognized where she was being led. This was the outdoor patio where she had once met with Stewart. It all seemed like some other life she'd lived. Someplace she wouldn't be going back to.

They exited the right side of the Davis mansion. More police cars than Brenda could count were everywhere, the red and blue lights swirling in the orange illumination of an angry fire out of control.

Brenda began to cough uncontrollably, struggling to keep down the smoky phlegm that gathered in her throat. Lisa came up from behind, took hold of Brenda's shoulders and guided her toward the front of the house. What met them there was a scene of lights, police cars, fire trucks and television station vans. Dozens of people were scurrying about, doing their jobs.

TPD cars were lined alongside the house, away from the front entrance, to allow the fire trucks access to the driveway. There must have been five trucks sitting in the circular drive. Lisa led her to an unmarked car that Brenda assumed was hers. "Sit down in the car. Put your head back and don't move. I'm going to find you some water." Lisa left.

In the distance, Brenda caught the sound of more sirens approaching and, overhead, the buzz of a helicopter. When she looked at the old Davis mansion, she saw the entire top floor completely engulfed in flames. Fingers of violent orange, yellow and white heat plunged upward from the roof.

It was hypnotizing to watch a fire eat. It was almost like a living, breathing beast, with many voices and faces. The sound of the Davis house burning was more like a hissing roar. Brenda watched in awe as the top part of the house caved into the bottom floor, the fire swallowing it. There was nothing she could do now. If Tina had been in that house, she was gone. But Brenda refused to believe that. Maybe one of the firefighters had found her.

The loud, piercing sirens of at least two more fire engines

broke Brenda's trance. They pulled up and surrounded what was left of the mansion.

Let it burn. She wanted to laugh. She felt the hysteria seeping through her system. She couldn't break down, not now. She had to find out what happened. She had to find Tina. She tried to get out of the squad car, but just as she did, Lisa shoved her back in. She had bottle of water in her hand.

"You're not going anywhere. Here, drink some of this." Lisa leaned down close into Brenda's face. "I'm going to have someone take you to the Tampa General ER. I want them to check out your lungs and back."

Brenda pushed her away. "I'm not leaving."

Lisa motioned for an officer. "Make sure she gets to TGH Emergency. Wait for her then drive her home. Get back with me."

Brenda knew Lisa was trying to do what was best, but how was she supposed to understand how Brenda felt? It wasn't someone Lisa loved who might have been trapped in that inferno.

She looked at Lisa with as much defiance as she could muster. "I'm not leaving until I know for sure."

Lisa sighed. "There was no one inside that house, Brenda. We checked it out before we discovered the elevator."

"Steven Selby was in that house."

"Steven Selby? Who the hell is Steven Selby?"

"The devil's apprentice, you could say. Works for Malenko. And the FBI."

Lisa shook her head. "Well, devil's apprentice or not, if he was still in there after we got out, he's just ashes."

The tears came like a flood and Brenda couldn't control them. She'd failed Tina like she'd failed Timmy. Why hadn't she been there for Tina when she got home? If she was given such special powers, why hadn't she been able to use them to save Timmy and find Tina?

She sobbed freely, allowing the pain in her heart to explode.

When the TPD officer started up the car, Lisa bent down and took Brenda's hands. "I'll check in on you tomorrow. You might want to stay with a friend or have someone come over to your place. I don't think you should be alone." She slammed the door shut on Brenda.

Brenda barely heard her. Timmy's screams and the screeching of the car before it hit him competed with the roar of flames to drown out everything else.

Chapter Twenty

It was almost like going through that tunnel during a near-death experience. She'd been there once, but this time, she hadn't died.

The thick fog that had blanketed her brain lifted and the sound of a woman's voice broke through, faintly at first, then more clearly. It was Cubbie.

"Hold on, I think she's awake now. I'll call you back."

Brenda opened her eyes and saw only a blob in the dim light. She blinked and rubbed her eyes softly. This time, her friend came into focus. Cubbie's big face was looking down at her.

"Well it's about time, sugar. They really knocked you out, didn't they?"

"Knocked me out?" Brenda struggled to sit up in bed. It was her bed and her room in Malfour. The light in the room was blinding. Cubbie had opened up all the shades and curtains.

"The hospital kept you there for hours. They X-rayed your

lungs. You're clean. Your back was pretty raw with burns. You'll have to keep those bandages on for a while. You were so agitated they pumped you up big-time with tranquilizers. Honey, you went out like a light. How are you feeling?"

"Cubbie, what are you doing here?"

"Your detective friend called last night. She said she went through your cell phone directory for my number. She didn't think you should be alone in a big house and all. I came over. Been here all night." Cubbie's face grew serious. "It was a horrible ordeal for you, sugar. Why don't you rest? Plenty of time to talk about things."

Brenda wanted out of the bed. She wasn't going to get anything accomplished laid up like this. "Cubbie, you've got to help me find out what happened to Tina." The memory of yesterday came pounding at her head. The longer she waited, the colder the trail to Tina and Malenko got.

Cubbie shook her head. "No, no. Detective Chambliss just called and said I was to make sure you didn't leave this house until she got here."

Brenda stared at her. "Lisa is coming now? Did she have any news?"

"I'm sorry, boss lady, she wouldn't tell me anything. She's coming to see you."

Encouraged by Lisa's impending visit and the hope that she might have news regarding Malenko or Tina, Brenda got up and slowly worked her way to the shower. The bright, clean walls made her stop in the middle of the hall. The stains that had cast shadows through the walls of Malfour were gone. What about Tina's workroom? Was the silhouette of her lover still glaring down from the wall?

Brenda inched toward the room.

"Boss lady, what's wrong?" Cubbie came up behind her.

Brenda waved her off. She opened the door wide. The shadowy image of Tina's head was gone.

Standing beside her, Cubbie looked around at the half-finished sculptures Tina had left behind. "Honey, I'm not so sure putting yourself through this is going to help you at all. Come on, why don't we go downstairs and I can fix us some breakfast." She started toward the door.

Brenda ignored her. She tried to remember what Susan Christie had told her about Malfour and Brenda's ability to communicate with the house. Had Malfour been trying to show her what was about to happen? Were her dreams of guillotines, blood and violence all signs of things to come? And Tina's head on the wall of her studio, had that been the final warning?

She stood very still, trying to reach out and understand why she wasn't able to communicate with Tina. Brenda refused to believe Tina was dead. Otherwise she would know it. Feel it. She had no proof and therefore still trusted that Tina was alive and no doubt being held against her will by Malenko. And it was up to Brenda to find her.

By the time Brenda finished her sponge bath and dressed, Lisa was ringing the doorbell downstairs. Cubbie had already left. Brenda had to practically shove her out the door, but not before promising to call her every day. She didn't feel like she needed a babysitter. She was sure Cubbie had better things to do than watch her eat and sleep.

Brenda bounded down the stairs and opened the door. Lisa was in somber garb—brown pants, royal blue blouse and a black suede jacket. She looked a hell of a lot better than she had last night. But the Buddha-like smile was missing from her face.

"Mind if I come in, Brenda?"

Brenda suddenly felt herself flush. She opened the door for her. "I've been waiting for you."

Lisa rubbed the back of her neck, then stuck her hands in her pockets. She was uncomfortable about something. Brenda had never seen her like this.

Lisa's gaze locked on Brenda's. "How are you feeling? You had quite a night."

161

Brenda mustered a smile for her. The woman probably saved her life. "A little sick to my stomach, some burns on my back, but otherwise, I got a clean bill of health." She felt a bit embarrassed. Last night had been a test of strength. She wasn't sure she passed. "Listen, Lisa, I have to apologize for my breakdown last night."

Lisa shook her head. "No, don't."

Brenda couldn't wait any longer. The shivers went through her body, tiny goose bumps erupting on her arms. "Did they find anything after the fire? Any news?" She couldn't face asking the direct question.

Lisa kept staring at her. She said evenly, "That's why I'm here." She glanced toward the living room. "You might want to sit down."

That's when Brenda saw a shadowy form appear behind Lisa. It seemed to be deep gray smoke, morphing into a human shape but with no distinct features, except for the darker areas that represented the long hair.

"Tina," she whispered. Her whole body felt deflated, like a punctured balloon. Sensations of hot and cold swept through her inner core. Small beads of sweat dotted her face. She knew who this shape was.

"Brenda?" Lisa glanced behind her and then moved toward Brenda. "What's wrong? Are you okay?"

Brenda struggled to remain standing. When she opened her mouth, nothing came out.

"Can I get you some water? Where's your kitchen?"

"No." Brenda put out a hand. The shape behind Lisa slowly rose into the air, never fully materializing, then disappeared.

Brenda remembered the same image of her mother at the grave site the day they buried her. Her mother's spirit had been merely a shadow caught between the worlds, as if making a last attempt to say good-bye.

"You found her." Brenda stopped short of tears.

Lisa stared at her, confused. "There was nothing in the house. Very little was left that we could use. But . . ." She paused. "Brenda,

I've tried to figure out how to tell you. We found two bodies a short distance from the house in some mangroves." She hesitated, clearly at a loss. "They—"

"They were decapitated," Brenda finished. She knew.

"We were able to identify them. One was an Arthur Clemens, the other . . ." She glanced away. "I'm sorry, Brenda."

There was a loud buzzing in Brenda's ears as the room began to fade to a dull gray. Her heart was thumping so hard in her chest, she thought it might burst through. She leaned back against one of the foyer tables.

Lisa rushed forward and put a steady arm around her. "I think you should have Cubbie stay with you for a while, Brenda. It isn't a good time for you to be alone."

Brenda walked to door and opened it wide. "Thank you for your concern, detective. I think being alone is exactly what I deserve." She motioned for Lisa to leave.

"Brenda, take time to grieve. It's a natural process, then call me if you need me."

Brenda shut the door on her, turned and screamed, "Carlotta. Angelique. Help me."

Chapter Twenty-one

"Ashes to ashes, dust to dust." The priest spoke in a soft voice to the large crowd of mourners at the old Bronx cemetery.

Brenda tuned out his voice and gazed out at the people who huddled together in the drab colors of death. Tina lay in the bronze-colored coffin that gleamed in the sun. There were so many young faces she didn't recognize. Were they students from the art institute?

The Marchanti family was a large one, and they stood together in a tight line, like soldiers, keeping Tina's mother steady. It had been hard for Brenda to swallow the tears when she spoke to Mrs. Marchanti about Tina.

Her father stood beside her, one hand resting on her back. Brenda felt for him. He'd had to bury her mother three months ago and now she had dragged him here. To surround himself with more death and suffering again. Guilt slivered its way through

Brenda like a venomous snake. She was responsible for Tina's death.

But she couldn't dwell on Tina. There was no way of thinking about her without gruesome images shoving their way into the memories. And then there was the persistent guilt. Dear God, she'd never had a chance to say good-bye. The only thing Brenda felt was numb.

A loud cry of grief pierced her thoughts. Tina's mother was screaming and trying to pull away from her husband's grasp. The priest sprinkled holy water on the coffin and with a slight jerk, the coffin began to descend into the ground.

Her father squeezed her hand. "You okay, sweetheart?"

Brenda looked deep into her dad's eyes. He wasn't back in February with her mother, he was here with her. She squeezed back. "I'm okay, Dad."

Brenda hugged her father one more time at the Delta entrance to LaGuardia Airport. Her flight back to Tampa was boarding in two hours.

"Remember, sweetheart, if you need me to come down and stay for a while, let me know. And your room hasn't changed since you left Monte Point. It's there for you."

"I have friends who'll keep me company." The ghosts will always be there, she thought. All of them.

Her father waved good-bye as she turned to the curbside attendant examining her tickets in order to check her bag. Her father stopped her. "Oh, Brenda, did you get that box I sent you?"

"It was Mother's diary."

Her father looked at her in mild surprise as she smiled, tipped the attendant and went inside.

Epilogue

Nancy Winters Strange diary, June 24th, 1981
It makes me satisfied to watch Raymond and Brenda together. She needs at least one of us to be there for her. I have distanced myself from her even further. She'll never replace my Timmy. Raymond feels I'm neglecting her. Well, I am. He wants us all to go as a family to see some shrink. I won't go. There's nothing wrong with me. I'm the normal one. Brenda is the freak. And it isn't just about Timmy's absence, it's about Brenda herself. She frightens me. I was jealous at first about not being gifted with the Winters psychic ability, but now, seeing what she's going through, I'm glad I was spared. Sometimes, Brenda isn't in the present. I don't know where she is, but she isn't here with us. The older she gets, the deeper she goes into whatever little world she has going on in her head. She spends all her time reading, or watching science fiction television shows. It just isn't healthy. I tried to get her more involved in other activities, but she shrinks back into her books. Maybe she'll be a lawyer or doctor. Raymond has high hopes for her. I have little. My daughter will

suffer. I know she will. She won't understand what everything going on in her head will mean. Without the guidance of the other Winters women, she'll be a cripple unable to use her gift.

I hope one day my daughter will forgive me.

Publications from
BELLA BOOKS, INC.
The best in contemporary lesbian fiction

P.O. Box 10543, Tallahassee, FL 32302
Phone: 800-729-4992
www.bellabooks.com

WHEN LOVE FINDS A HOME by Megan Carter. 280 pp. What will it take for Anna and Rona to find their way back to each other again? 1-59493-041-4 $12.95

MEMORIES TO DIE FOR by Adrian Gold. 240pp. Rachel Katz, a forensic psychologist, attempts to avoid her attraction to the charms of Anna Sigurdson. Will Anna's persistence and patience get her past Rachel's fears of a broken heart? 1-59493-038-4 $12.95

SILENT HEART by Claire McNab. 280 pp. Exotic lesbian romance. 1-59493-044-9 $12.95

MIDNIGHT RAIN by Peggy J. Herring. 240 pp. Bridget McBee is determined to find the woman who saved her life. 1-59493-021-X $12.95

THE MISSING PAGE A Brenda Strange Mystery by Patty G. Henderson. 240 pp. Brenda investigates her client's murder . . . 1-59493-004-X $12.95

WHISPERS ON THE WIND by Frankie J. Jones. 240 pp. Dixon thinks she and her best friend, Elizabeth Colter, would make the perfect couple . . . 1-59493-037-6 $12.95

CALL OF THE DARK: EROTIC LESBIAN TALES OF THE SUPERNATURAL edited by Therese Szymanski—from Bella After Dark. 320 pp. 1-59493-040-6 $14.95

A TIME TO CAST AWAY A Helen Black Mystery by Pat Welch. 240 pp. Helen stops by Alice's apartment—only to find the woman dead . . . 1-59493-036-8 $12.95

DESERT OF THE HEART by Jane Rule. 224 pp. The book that launched the most popular lesbian movie of all time is back. 1-1-59493-035-X $12.95

THE NEXT WORLD by Ursula Steck. 240 pp. Anna's friend Mido is threatened and eventually disappears . . . 1-59493-024-4 $12.95

CALL SHOTGUN by Jaime Clevenger. 240 pp. Kelly gets pulled back into the world of private investigation . . . 1-59493-016-3 $12.95

52 PICKUP by Bonnie J. Morris and E.B. Casey. 240 pp. 52 hot, romantic tales—one for every Saturday night of the year. 1-59493-026-0 $12.95

GOLD FEVER by Lyn Denison. 240 pp. Kate's first love, Ashley, returns to their home town, where Kate now lives . . . 1-1-59493-039-2 $12.95

RISKY INVESTMENT by Beth Moore. 240 pp. Lynn's best friend and roommate needs her to pretend Chris is his fiancé. But nothing is ever easy. 1-59493-019-8 $12.95

HUNTER'S WAY by Gerri Hill. 240 pp. Homicide detective Tori Hunter is forced to team up with the hot-tempered Samantha Kennedy. 1-59493-018-X $12.95

CAR POOL by Karin Kallmaker. 240 pp. Soft shoulders, merging traffic and slippery when wet . . . Anthea and Shay find love in the car pool. 1-59493-013-9 $12.95

NO SISTER OF MINE by Jeanne G'Fellers. 240 pp. Telepathic women fight to coexist with a patriarchal society that wishes their eradication. ISBN 1-59493-017-1 $12.95

ON THE WINGS OF LOVE by Megan Carter. 240 pp. Stacie's reporting career is on the rocks. She has to interview bestselling author Cheryl, or else! ISBN 1-59493-027-9 $12.95

WICKED GOOD TIME by Diana Tremain Braund. 224 pp. Does Christina need Miki as a protector . . . or want her as a lover? ISBN 1-59493-031-7 $12.95

THOSE WHO WAIT by Peggy J. Herring. 240 pp. Two brilliant sisters—in love with the same woman! ISBN 1-59493-032-5 $12.95

ABBY'S PASSION by Jackie Calhoun. 240 pp. Abby's bipolar sister helps turn her world upside down, so she must decide what's most important. ISBN 1-59493-014-7 $12.95

PICTURE PERFECT by Jane Vollbrecht. 240 pp. Kate is reintroduced to Casey, the daughter of an old friend. Can they withstand Kate's career? ISBN 1-59493-015-5 $12.95

PAPERBACK ROMANCE by Karin Kallmaker. 240 pp. Carolyn falls for tall, dark and . . . female . . . in this classic lesbian romance. ISBN 1-59493-033-3 $12.95

DAWN OF CHANGE by Gerri Hill. 240 pp. Susan ran away to find peace in remote Kings Canyon—then she met Shawn . . . ISBN 1-59493-011-2 $12.95

DOWN THE RABBIT HOLE by Lynne Jamneck. 240 pp. Is a killer holding a grudge against FBI Agent Samantha Skellar? ISBN 1-59493-012-0 $12.95

SEASONS OF THE HEART by Jackie Calhoun. 240 pp. Overwhelmed, Sara saw only one way out—leaving . . . ISBN 1-59493-030-9 $12.95

TURNING THE TABLES by Jessica Thomas. 240 pp. The 2nd Alex Peres Mystery. *From ghosties and ghoulies and long leggity beasties* . . . ISBN 1-59493-009-0 $12.95

FOR EVERY SEASON by Frankie Jones. 240 pp. Andi, who is investigating a 65-year-old murder, meets Janice, a charming district attorney . . . ISBN 1-59493-010-4 $12.95

LOVE ON THE LINE by Laura DeHart Young. 240 pp. Kay leaves a younger woman behind to go on a mission to Alaska . . . will she regret it? ISBN 1-59493-008-2 $12.95

UNDER THE SOUTHERN CROSS by Claire McNab. 200 pp. Lee, an American travel agent, goes down under and meets Australian Alex, and the sparks fly under the Southern Cross. ISBN 1-59493-029-5 $12.95

SUGAR by Karin Kallmaker. 240 pp. Three women want sugar from Sugar, who can't make up her mind. ISBN 1-59493-001-5 $12.95

FALL GUY by Claire McNab. 200 pp. 16th Detective Inspector Carol Ashton Mystery. ISBN 1-59493-000-7 $12.95

ONE SUMMER NIGHT by Gerri Hill. 232 pp. Johanna swore to never fall in love again—but then she met the charming Kelly . . . ISBN 1-59493-007-4 $12.95

TALK OF THE TOWN TOO by Saxon Bennett. 181 pp. Second in the series about wild and fun loving friends. ISBN 1-931513-77-5 $12.95

LOVE SPEAKS HER NAME by Laura DeHart Young. 170 pp. Love and friendship, desire and intrigue, spark this exciting sequel to *Forever and the Night*. ISBN 1-59493-002-3 $12.95

TO HAVE AND TO HOLD by Peggy J. Herring. 184 pp. By finally letting down her defenses, will Dorian be opening herself to a devastating betrayal?
ISBN 1-59493-005-8 $12.95

WILD THINGS by Karin Kallmaker. 228 pp. Dutiful daughter Faith has met the perfect man. There's just one problem: she's in love with his sister. ISBN 1-931513-64-3 $12.95

SHARED WINDS by Kenna White. 216 pp. Can Emma rebuild more than just Lanny's marina?
ISBN 1-59493-006-6 $12.95

THE UNKNOWN MILE by Jaime Clevenger. 253 pp. Kelly's world is getting more and more complicated every moment.
ISBN 1-931513-57-0 $12.95

TREASURED PAST by Linda Hill. 189 pp. A shared passion for antiques leads to love.
ISBN 1-59493-003-1 $12.95

SIERRA CITY by Gerri Hill. 284 pp. Chris and Jesse cannot deny their growing attraction . . .
ISBN 1-931513-98-8 $12.95

ALL THE WRONG PLACES by Karin Kallmaker. 174 pp. Sex and the single girl—Brandy is looking for love and usually she finds it. Karin Kallmaker's first *After Dark* erotic novel.
ISBN 1-931513-76-7 $12.95

WHEN THE CORPSE LIES A Motor City Thriller by Therese Szymanski. 328 pp. Butch bad-girl Brett Higgins is used to waking up next to beautiful women she hardly knows. Problem is, this one's dead.
ISBN 1-931513-74-0 $12.95

GUARDED HEARTS by Hannah Rickard. 240 pp. Someone's reminding Alyssa about her secret past, and then she becomes the suspect in a series of burglaries.
ISBN 1-931513-99-6 $12.95

ONCE MORE WITH FEELING by Peggy J. Herring. 184 pp. Lighthearted, loving, romantic adventure.
ISBN 1-931513-60-0 $12.95

TANGLED AND DARK A Brenda Strange Mystery by Patty G. Henderson. 240 pp. When investigating a local death, Brenda finds two possible killers—one diagnosed with Multiple Personality Disorder.
ISBN 1-931513-75-9 $12.95

WHITE LACE AND PROMISES by Peggy J. Herring. 240 pp. Maxine and Betina realize sex may not be the most important thing in their lives. ISBN 1-931513-73-2 $12.95

UNFORGETTABLE by Karin Kallmaker. 288 pp. Can Rett find love with the cheerleader who broke her heart so many years ago?
ISBN 1-931513-63-5 $12.95

HIGHER GROUND by Saxon Bennett. 280 pp. A delightfully complex reflection of the successful, high society lives of a small group of women. ISBN 1-931513-69-4 $12.95

LAST CALL A Detective Franco Mystery by Baxter Clare. 240 pp. Frank overlooks all else to try to solve a cold case of two murdered children . . . ISBN 1-931513-70-8 $12.95

ONCE UPON A DYKE: NEW EXPLOITS OF FAIRY-TALE LESBIANS by Karin Kallmaker, Julia Watts, Barbara Johnson & Therese Szymanski. 320 pp. You've never read fairy tales like these before! From Bella After Dark. ISBN 1-931513-71-6 $14.95

FINEST KIND OF LOVE by Diana Tremain Braund. 224 pp. Can Molly and Carolyn stop clashing long enough to see beyond their differences? ISBN 1-931513-68-6 $12.95

DREAM LOVER by Lyn Denison. 188 pp. A soft, sensuous, romantic fantasy.
ISBN 1-931513-96-1 $12.95